Numbe

MW00414774

Sage Gardens Cozy Mystery Series

Cindy Bell

Copyright © 2016 Cindy Bell

All rights reserved.

ISBN-13: 978-1530502516

ISBN-10: 1530502519

Table of Contents

Chapter One

Just as the hero was about to put in the final number to break the code, a sound stirred Walt from the fantasy world he'd disappeared into. He tried to ignore it at first, but the shrill ring of his cell phone caused him to lose his place on the page. He grimaced and grabbed for his phone. He'd been meaning to change the ringtone to something less jarring, but he only remembered when the phone rang and by the time he got off the phone he had forgotten. The number illuminated on the screen was not familiar to him. He hesitated to answer, but his curiosity won out.

"Hello? This is Walt."

"Walter Right?"

"Yes, this is he. May I help you with something?"

"Are you familiar with a man named Lawrence Magnus?"

"Magnus? Yes." Walt frowned as he recalled the man. "It's been quite some time since I've seen him though."

"Exactly how long?" The tone of the man's voice became sterner.

Walt sat forward in his chair and narrowed his eyes. "What is this all about? Who are you?"

"My name is Detective Jenson. I am investigating Mr. Magnus' death."

"Death? Oh dear, I didn't know he had passed." Walt closed his eyes as the minutes and seconds he'd carefully calculated until his own expected demise flashed through his mind. The clock always kept moving.

"It happened last night. That is why I'm calling."

"Well, it is a shame that he is dead, but I'm not sure how I can help. Like I said, I haven't seen him in years."

"I think you can help." His brusque tone held Walt's attention. "In fact, I'm sure you can."

"I'd be glad to. Just tell me how you think I can help."

"First you could explain to me why Magnus died with a pen in his hand, and a piece of paper beside him that had your name on it."

"My name?"

"Walter Right. That's your name isn't it?"

"Well yes, but I don't have any idea why he would have written down my name."

"There must be a reason, don't you think? A dying man took the time to write down your name."

"Of course, logically there must be a reason. I just don't know what that reason is."

"You had no recent contact with Magnus?"

"No I didn't. He was my boss at one point, that was all. We weren't even friends. I came in, I did my job, and he paid me. I don't think we exchanged anything more than good morning or good night."

3

"Maybe you will remember more when we speak to you about the murder in person."

"I won't. I haven't seen or spoken to him in years. I'm sorry. I wish I could help you."

"I'm sure that you do. We'll be in touch."

Walt gripped the phone tight. "Detective, really..."

He realized the line was dead. He lowered the phone and stared into space for a moment. It slowly set in that this was no mistake. His old boss was dead, and the police planned to speak to him because he was a suspect. What if they decided to arrest him? What if there was no way to avoid going to jail? His stomach sank as he thought of being forced into a filthy, small cell with an open toilet and several other men. As a wave of dizziness washed over him he realized that his breathing was out of control. He gasped for air and dialed the number of the only person he thought might be able to help. His friend Eddy was a retired detective, and would at least be able to give him an idea of how much trouble he might be in. Eddy answered right away.

"Walt, good morning."

Walt gulped back another breath and managed to form a few words. "Eddy, I need your help please. Can you come over?"

"Of course I can. What's wrong? Are you okay?"

"I'm not sure, please hurry."

"I'll be right there."

Walt struggled to take a slow, deep breath. It was impossible. His breathing pattern was already off. He had to calm down if he wanted to breathe normally. He walked into the kitchen and over to a drawer. He opened the drawer to find a brown, paper bag neatly lying right in place. He picked up the bag. He hung up the phone with Eddy and closed the bag over his nose and mouth. With every breath in and out he tried to focus on being calm. However, even the crinkle of the paper bag was enough to make him jump. How would he keep himself clean in jail? Communal showers? Another wave of dizziness caused his knees to nearly buckle. He closed his eyes and tried to focus on the solution. If Magnus wrote down his name, there must have been a reason. Maybe he thought that Walt would be able to help him in some way.

As Walt slowed his breaths he tried to recall what work he had done for Magnus. His primary project was to install and customize a program on the computer system. Walt remembered walking Magnus through the process and writing down some notes for him. But that was at least fifteen years ago. Why would he write down his name? Maybe he thought he should call him? But for what? It was not as if Walt was some highly trained assassin, or even the slightest bit trained. His expertise was in numbers, and that was rarely related to murder.

Walt recalled Magnus as not being the friendliest person. In fact he was quite cruel to some of his employees, but no more so than many of the other high-powered CEOs Walt had dealt with. Magnus had the ability to make a dream come true, or ruin a life, and he wasn't shy about doing either. Maybe his behavior had angered the wrong person. But that still didn't explain why he would want to involve Walt in his murder. He shook his head and focused on breathing. When there was a heavy knock at the door he nearly jumped out of his skin. Walt kept the paper bag over his nose and mouth as he hurried to answer the door. He assumed it was Eddy, but he couldn't be sure. When he opened the door he breathed a sigh of relief, which made the brown, paper bag expand with a snap.

Eddy stared at him with wide eyes. "Walt, are you okay, Buddy? Do you need a medic?" He stepped inside and closed the door behind him. Walt lowered the bag.

"No, I think I'm okay. I'm trying to prevent a full blown panic attack. This bag is not helping!" He crushed the paper bag and tossed it on the floor. A second later he snatched it up and began to smooth out the wrinkles he had caused.

"Why don't you just sit down for a second and tell me what's happened?" Eddy gestured towards Walt's favorite chair. Once Walt sat down, Eddy sat down across from him.

"My old boss is dead. He was murdered!"

"Okay," Eddy said thoughtfully, "but I'm not quite sure what to make of that. I'm sorry for your loss, but how does it involve you? Were you two close?"

"Not at all. It doesn't involve me at all, well it shouldn't. For some reason Magnus wrote down my name on a piece of paper just before he died. Why would he do that?" He shook his head and stared down at the floor.

"I don't know. You're the one that needs to answer that question." Eddy frowned. "Any ideas?"

"No, none at all. We weren't even friends when I worked for him."

"Do you think he might have meant a

different Walt?" Eddy lifted his hat to scratch the top of his head. "It seems odd to me that he would be so determined to write down your name with no recent contact."

"My name may be fairly common, but I doubt he knew another Walter Right. He wrote down my full name. I suppose it's possible that he knew another Walter Right, but clearly the police don't think there is another one that he could be referring to." Walt cringed. "I think the police see it as him naming his killer. I really think they are going to be coming after me."

"Yes, they probably will."

"What?" Walt looked up at him with wide eyes. "I thought you were supposed to be helping me here? How is that helping?"

"I'm just telling you the truth, Walt. They are going to want to question you. Any detective would. If there's a chance that the victim named his killer it has to be followed up on."

"This is not making me feel any better at all."

Walt shook his head.

"I'm just trying to be honest with you, Walt. It's better to know what to expect than to worry about it."

"I'm going to worry about it whether or not I know what to expect."

"Look, they'll question you, and as long as there is nothing concerning, they will be on their way."

"What would be concerning?"

"Well, any conflict you might have had with this man. Any evidence of recent contact that you do not admit to. Lying, is a big one."

"I'm not lying. I haven't spoken to this man in years. Why would I lie about that?"

"I don't think you're lying. But I'm not the one who matters here. The detectives are. If you talk to them with a paper bag on your face you're not exactly going to be screaming calm, innocent man. Understand?"

"Okay, okay." Walt drew a deep breath and tried to lower the paper bag. His heart raced and he squished it tighter against his face. "I don't think I can do this."

Eddy reached out and put a hand on Walt's shoulder. "You're going to have to. I can get you through this, Walt, but you have to trust me."

Walt nodded a little. He lowered the paper bag. "Are you sure you can? What if they arrest me? What if they put me in handcuffs? What if they put me in the backseat of a dirty police car?"

"Listen, I'm going to be here with you. You've done nothing wrong. There's no reason to be concerned about being arrested. The important thing is to make sure that you are honest with the detectives. Now, are you sure that there is nothing in your past with Magnus that would be of concern to a detective?"

Walt frowned. He thought back to the first few times he had met with Magnus. "Well, to be honest, I almost refused to work for him."

"Why is that?"

"He financed large companies, but he also had a reputation for stealing, corporate style. He would buy struggling companies at a pittance and then restructure them to be part of larger, established companies by getting rid of most of the staff in the process and replacing some of them with young, cheap labor. It wasn't against the law, I just found it morally wrong."

"Did that upset you?"

"Well, I'm a numbers guy, but I hate to see small companies gutted before they ever have a proper chance." Walt shook his head. "But business was business to me, and he was a big client. So, I just ignored his reputation and went with it."

"Hm. That could be something." Eddy narrowed his eyes.

"What do you mean that could be something?" Walt raised an eyebrow. "It could be something bad?"

"Having an objection to the man's morals could be skewed as motive. They might make the case that you were stewing all these years over his behavior and decided to finally do something about it."

"That's ridiculous."

"To you and me it is, but to a detective grasping at straws it might be enough to make a case on. Unless they bring it up, I wouldn't mention it."

"What if they do bring it up?" Walt's eyes widened. Before Eddy could answer there was a knock on the door. Walt gulped and began to gasp for air. He put the paper bag back to his face. Eddy shook his head. Reluctantly, Walt put the paper bag down on the table beside the couch. He walked over to the door and opened it. Just as he feared there were two people on the other side of the door, a man and a woman. The man flashed a badge at him.

"Detective Jenson. We spoke on the phone?"

"Yes." Walt nodded. "I already told you what I know."

"I'd just like to go over a few things with you. May we come inside?" He looked over at his partner, a younger woman, who stared hard at Walt.

"Yes, of course. Uh, if you wouldn't mind just wiping your feet." Walt pointed to the sign beside the door that politely requested guests to wipe their feet. Detective Jenson rolled his eyes, but wiped his feet. His partner did the same. Walt watched the menial effort they offered. His fingers itched to get the broom from the kitchen. But he controlled himself and resisted the urge. Eddy remained right beside Walt as the two detectives stepped inside.

"This is my friend, Eddy." Walt glanced over at him. Eddy nodded at the detectives and offered his hand. Each took it in a mild shake. From the annoyance in Detective Jenson's eyes, Eddy guessed that he would have preferred to speak to Walt alone.

14

"We're just trying to get a handle on what happened to Magnus. Obviously there is a reason he wrote your name down on that piece of paper."

"There must be, but I don't know what that reason is. Like I told you on the phone, I haven't seen him in so long. I probably wouldn't even recognize him if I saw him."

The female detective produced a photograph. Eddy noticed that Detective Jenson didn't introduce her. He knew why. The detective wanted to keep Walt off balance, uncertain of what her role was. It was a well-used method in police work. "You might not remember him, Mr. Right, but he certainly remembered you."

Walt stared at the photograph. His body shivered in reaction to the eyes he recognized, but a much older visage that could have been a stranger on the street. Now he was dead.

"How did he die?"

"One swift blow to the head." Detective Jenson narrowed his eyes. "It was quick."

15

"That's good at least." Walt shook his head.

"Is it?" Detective Jenson raised an eyebrow. "Do you know how much strength it would take to deliver a blow like that?"

"I would assume quite a bit. I'd need more information to calculate an exact amount." Walt met his eyes.

"You're that interested?" The female detective stepped closer to him. "Do you find something interesting about death?"

"No, not at all. I just have a mind for numbers." He frowned and looked over at Eddy. Eddy narrowed his eyes.

"When was the victim killed?" Eddy asked.

"Victim?" Detective Jenson turned his attention on Eddy. He studied him for a moment before he spoke again. "Mr. Magnus was killed between eight and ten o'clock last night."

"There you have it. Walt was with me during that time. There's no way he could have been involved."

"I hadn't made any accusations." Detective Jenson snapped his attention back to Walt. "Should I? Your friend here seems awful quick to provide you with an alibi."

Walt stared back. His voice caught in his throat. Eddy interrupted his stuttering.

"That's because it's true. We shared dinner and drinks at a new restaurant. I'm sure that Walt has the receipt to prove it. He always keeps his receipts."

"I do." Walt nodded. "Can I get it?"

"Sure, go right ahead." Detective Jenson sighed.

Walt walked over to his desk. The moment he had his back turned Detective Jenson locked eyes with Eddy.

"You've known Walt long?"

"A few years."

"Then you didn't know him when he worked for Mr. Magnus?"

17

"No, I didn't," Eddy said.

"Here it is." Walt turned around and held out a slip of paper to Detective Jenson. "It has the time. I'm sure that the staff would be willing to speak to you to confirm our presence."

"Let's see." Detective Jenson studied the small slip of paper for far longer than it should have taken to read it. He nodded and looked at Walt. "You work in finance?"

"I used to, I'm retired."

Detective Jenson tucked the receipt into his pocket.

"I'll need a copy of that." Walt looked at him anxiously.

"One will be provided," the detective said. "We appreciate your cooperation, Mr. Right. Please understand that at this time we can't clear you as a person of interest. It would be best if you remained in the immediate area in case we need to reach you for further questioning."

"Of course I understand." Walt stood up from

the couch and shook the detective's hand.

"I don't." Eddy looked at him with annoyance. "He provided you a receipt which confirms his alibi. There shouldn't need to be any further questioning."

"And exactly who are you again?" Detective Jenson furrowed his brow as he looked at Eddy.

"I'm a friend."

"Oh? Not a lawyer?"

"No." Eddy tightened his lips. The female detective leaned close to Detective Jenson and whispered in his ear. Eddy tensed as Detective Jenson's expression shifted from impatience to exasperation.

"I see. You're retired police. Fine, I'm sure you think you know everything about this case. You should know better than anyone how important it is to follow the clues, especially those left behind by the victim himself. Perhaps if you were a little less concerned with showing off in front of your friend and a little more concerned with justice, this meeting could have been more productive."

"Or maybe if you were questioning the right suspect, you would have already solved it." Eddy folded his arms across his chest.

"Mr. Right, we'll be in touch." Detective Jenson led his partner towards the door. Walt's eyes widened as the pair stepped out through the door. He sank back down onto the couch and tried to steady his breath.

"It's all right, Walt, they don't have anything on you. Just try to relax."

"I'm trying." Walt looked up at him. "But that detective looked very determined to see me in handcuffs."

"You're the easiest target. He wants you to be guilty so that he can close his case and go home to dinner. Hopefully he's an honest enough detective that he will not try to force a charge against you. He has to know from your alibi that you were not involved."

"I had no idea there were so many ifs before

we started solving cases with Jo and Samantha. I always used to assume that if you're innocent, you're innocent, if you're guilty, you're guilty, but clearly there is a lot more that goes into it than that."

Eddy squinted. "There shouldn't be, but yes there usually is."

"Do you really think they have no case?"

"Yes. But to be sure, let me check in with one of my contacts. Why don't you make us some tea?"

"Okay, yes, I can do that." Walt made his way into the kitchen.

As Eddy watched Walt walk away he hoped that he would be able to keep his friend out of jail.

Chapter Two

Eddy dialed a lab tech who was one of his most valuable police contacts. They had a bond that had been formed from a mutual need to see justice served even if it meant breaking the rules, occasionally. Eddy leaned against the wall and stared into space as he waited for Chris to pick up the phone. Sometimes the young man was occupied, and sometimes he just waited a while to see if whoever was on the line would hang up. Eddy knew him well enough to wait until the very last ring.

"Hello?"

"Chris, it's me Eddy."

"Oh Eddy. Sorry for the wait. I've got this detective all over me for some results that I told him wouldn't be in until tomorrow and he just won't give up."

"I understand. Actually, I'm calling to see if you can do me a favor."

"I'm pretty sure I already knew that." Chris gave a short laugh.

"Very perceptive, Chris."

"What case is it?"

"The Magnus murder."

"Oh right, that's a hot topic today. Someone else is assigned to it though. Why are you so interested?"

"You're not going to believe this."

"Try me."

"Apparently Magnus wrote my friend Walt's name down on a piece of paper before he was killed. The detective on the case, Detective Jenson, is considering it a dying declaration."

"Wow. If I didn't know who you were I wouldn't believe you, Eddy. Does Walt know the guy?"

"They worked together a long time ago. But Walt has no idea why he would write his name down. He's very nervous about the situation though. I think the only way I'm going to be able to get him to calm down is if I have some idea of what the detective might have against him. I doubt it could be much, because obviously he wasn't at the crime scene he was with me, but anything you can tell me would help me handle the situation."

"I understand." Chris paused a moment. Eddy detected the hesitation in his pause.

"What is it, Chris?"

"This is a high profile case, Eddy. Magnus was one of the elite of the city, and everyone is going to have their hands in this cookie jar. I'm just warning you that if you get too close you might face some serious consequences."

"I'm not afraid. I'll do whatever it takes to make sure Walt's name is cleared."

"I'll see what I can find out and give you a call back."

"Thanks Chris."

"Anything for you, Eddy, you know that."

"This one is for Walt. Keep that in mind. He doesn't deserve to be faced with any of this."

"I'm on it, Eddy, don't worry."

Eddy hung up the phone just as Walt stepped back into the room with two mugs of tea. He looked at Eddy and his hands were trembling from anxiety.

"What did he say?"

"He said he's going to keep on top of anything that happens. We'll be as informed as any of the detectives on the case, trust me."

"Okay." Walt sighed and handed him a mug. "That does make me feel a little better."

"It'll be fine."

Walt sat down on the couch. Eddy sat down beside him. The two sipped their tea in silence. Walt set his mug down on the coffee table and looked up at Eddy.

"So, it's not a good idea for me to fly off to some foreign country? I'm considering it."

"No." Eddy locked eyes with him. "That's as good as an admission of guilt. Whether or not you would actually be able to make it out of the country I'm not sure, but you would never be able to come back without facing the courts. Our best course of action is to clear your name, Walt, and I'm not going to let you run away from a crime that you didn't commit."

"You're not the one who is at risk of a lifetime of communal showers, are you, Eddy?" Walt raised an eyebrow. "I would not do well in prison."

"No, Walt you certainly wouldn't. Which is exactly why you're not going to end up there. Understand?"

Walt nodded but couldn't meet Eddy's eyes. Eddy's cell phone rang just in time to break the tension that brewed in the room. He saw that it was Chris and picked it up right away.

"I found out some information for you. I confirmed the time of death is fixed between eight and ten, with the murder most likely taking place around nine. The deceased was killed by one hard blow to the back of the head with a blunt object of some kind, which was not recovered."

"What about the motive? Was it vengeance? Crime of passion?" Eddy asked.

"There is some evidence that the computer system was invaded. Specifically, a financial program. The current theory is that Magnus surprised the intruder."

"Are they certain it was a man?"

"Fairly, nothing can be ruled out at this stage. The blow was from behind so he might not have seen the person coming for him."

"And Walt, have they given up on trying to pin this on him?"

"No, I don't think so. The note is a big clue that isn't going to be easily dismissed," Chris said.

"Is it possible that he was trying to write some other name, or something else entirely?"

"No, I doubt it. The letters are rounded and

complete, actually very well written for a dying declaration. There is something of interest though. Walt's name wasn't the only thing written on the note. There was also a set of numbers."

"What are they?" Eddy snatched up a pen from his pocket and jotted down the numbers on the napkin that Walt gave him with his tea. "Thanks a lot, Chris. Keep me up to date."

"I will."

Eddy hung up the phone and turned to find Walt on the edge of his seat. "Well?"

"He didn't just write your name on the piece of paper. He also wrote four numbers. 6886. Does that mean anything to you?"

"No, not at all. It's not even one of my favorite numbers."

"You have favorite numbers?" Eddy shook his head. "No, never mind. Well, they must mean something."

"I have a few programs on my computer that I could run them through. Maybe they will spit something out." He sighed and sat down in front of his computer. "I just keep thinking about why he would use the last of his energy to scribble down my name. The only reason I can think of is that he wanted my help. But why me?"

"I don't know." Eddy rested one hand on the desk and leaned over Walt's shoulder as he entered the same four numbers into several different programs. "But if we figure it out, we'll probably have a good idea of what really happened to him."

"He was a very wealthy man. His business was nearly pure profit. I'm sure at his age there were plenty of people chomping at the bit to take over his position."

"Good point. He was likely a target of many. That's a place to start. Maybe we can pinpoint who would have the most to gain from the situation."

"You know who would be best at discovering that?" Walt looked up from the computer screen.

"Samantha." Eddy nodded. "I'll give her a

call."

"If you call Samantha you should really call Jo, too."

"I will." Eddy frowned and fished in his pocket for his phone. As he dialed Samantha's number he walked away from the computer desk. Samantha answered after a few rings.

"Morning Eddy, how are you?"

"I'm okay. Walt's not having a great day though."

"Walt? Why not?"

"He's had a visit from the police."

"How come?"

"It's a long story. Could you just come over to his villa?"

"Sure. I'll be there in a few minutes. Want me to call Jo?"

"Yes, that would be a good idea." Eddy hung up and looked over at Walt. "The recruits are lined up. You're going to be just fine." The four friends lived in the beautiful retirement community of Sage Gardens which meant that they were seldom further than a few minutes away from each other.

"I'm trying to believe that." Walt clenched his jaw. Eddy sat down beside him and rested his palm on his shoulder.

"We're all looking out for you, Walt. Your job is to think of any connection, any reason that he might have written down your name. If we can figure that out then we might be able to get somewhere."

"I'll try."

Chapter Three

A few minutes later Samantha was at the door. Eddy opened the door for her and she walked past him into Walt's villa. He looked past her out onto the walkway.

"Jo isn't with you?"

"No, she's tied up with something, but she told me to let her know if we need her." Samantha brushed her braided hair back over her shoulder and settled her gaze on Walt. He managed to look up at her with a slight nod.

"It's good to know that she's on call." Eddy nodded. He gestured for Samantha to sit, then filled her in on everything they knew so far. Walt didn't speak a word. He folded and refolded a tissue in his hand until it was so tiny that Samantha thought it had disappeared.

"Walt, how are you holding up?" Samantha asked. When he looked up at her, she met his eyes.

"I'm okay," Walt squeaked the words out.

"I think that we need to come up with a plan." Eddy balled up a fist and struck the top of his knee. "We're wasting time here."

"Well, the first step is to get as much information as we can. Our best witnesses are going to be anyone that was in the building at the time of the murder, as well as friends and family that might have had recent contact with Magnus."

"Good luck with that." Walt shook his head. "He wasn't a friendly man, from what I can remember."

"Well, time changes people. Maybe he'd softened in his old age. I'll see what I can find out. Do you mind if I use your computer?" Samantha asked.

"No, it's fine. There's some hand sanitizer on the desk." Walt offered.

"Thanks." Samantha smiled at him. She passed a look over at Eddy who cringed. Walt was not the type to survive even a night in jail. As she logged into his computer she began searching for any information she could find on Magnus. In her attempts she discovered that he had very few social media accounts, and those that he did have had very few connections on them. The only network she could find for him was business related and even that hadn't been maintained or updated in months. She made a few calls to people she suspected were family members, but two didn't answer and the third had no idea who Magnus was. She sighed as she hung up her phone and spun around in the chair to look at the two men in the room.

"I have to be honest here, I'm not having any luck so far. It seems to me that Magnus didn't have anyone that he was close to, at least not anyone obvious."

"The only way we're going to find out any reliable information is if we go in person." Eddy gripped his hat between his hands. "Playing phone tag is not going to get us anywhere."

"You're right." Walt nodded. "We can head

out first thing in the morning."

"Actually, I don't think that's a good idea." Eddy met his eyes. "I don't think that you should go."

"Why not?" Walt frowned. Samantha put a hand on his shoulder.

"Eddy's just looking out for you," she said. "As long as you remain a suspect in this case you need to keep your distance from it. If the detectives spot you sniffing around, it will only make things look worse for you. Eddy and I can slide under the radar." Samantha was used to covert operations from her days as a journalist.

"I don't know." Walt looked concerned. "I hate to think of the two of you getting wrapped up in all of this. What if they figure out that you're trying to help me?"

"Don't worry about that. We're not going to do anything to cast any more suspicion your way. Samantha and I will visit the company in the morning and find out what the reaction there is like. That might give us some idea of other suspects."

"Yes, it might." Walt stared down at his hands. "Because right now I might be the only one."

"You have a good alibi." Samantha squeezed his shoulder. "Don't worry, Walt, all of this will be over soon enough."

"Before I'm in handcuffs?" He looked up at her warily.

"Absolutely." She leaned down and kissed his cheek. "You're in good hands, remember?"

Walt nodded, but he still didn't smile.

"I'll walk you out," Eddy said as he walked towards the door of Walt's villa. Samantha followed after him. The tension in the room followed as well. As soon as they were outside the door Eddy caught her elbow. "You shouldn't have told him that."

"What?"

"That he has nothing to worry about and we could keep him out of handcuffs."

"Isn't that the plan?" Samantha searched his eyes.

"Of course it is, but we can't promise that."

"Look, Walt is going to worry about it no matter what I say. I hope it makes him feel a little better that I'm confident we can help him. What's wrong with that?"

"Nothing is wrong with it, I just don't think that we should lie to him." Eddy gritted his teeth. "I wouldn't want to be lied to."

"Then let's not." She smiled a little. "Let's solve this case before handcuffs get anywhere near Walt."

Eddy sighed and settled his hat back on the top of his head. "That's easy to say, but not so easy to do, Samantha."

"With the four of us working together, I am certain we'll get to the bottom of this."

"As always your optimism is refreshing." He adjusted his hat. "I'll pick you up at eight tomorrow morning."

"I'll be ready."

Eddy watched as she walked away.

Samantha did her best to keep her step light and her attitude positive. But she didn't disagree with Eddy. Maybe her promise to Walt really would turn out to be a lie. But she would try her hardest to prevent that.

Eddy walked towards his villa. He wondered if it was the right thing to do to leave Walt alone, but he knew that the man appreciated his privacy. He decided to make a few more calls to a few more contacts. If there was anything that he could do to help Walt, he would do it.

***

Alone in his villa, Walt had yet to get off the

couch. He knew that he should. There were things that he could and should be doing, but he couldn't think of a single one. His mind buzzed with a vague panic that wasn't strong enough to make him lose it, but was just enough to prevent lucid thought. After a few minutes had passed he forced himself to stand up. Eddy was right, he was the only one that could figure out why Magnus wrote down his name. Luckily he kept records of everything.

Walt went back through boxes of files and folders until he found the one that he had collected during the time he had worked for Magnus. All of his financial records were kept there, along with other things as well. He looked over the job description and saw that he was working with a Chad Hillwick and a Len Lazario at the time. He remembered that although they worked in the same department they worked in different areas. Both Chad and Len were quite good friends and had become friendly with Walt in as far as they would occasionally have a coffee at work and discuss the different accounting systems in place. Becoming friends with people at work, or anyone for that matter, was unusual for Walt. They all left the company around the same time due to different reasons.

Sometimes Walt would keep small reminders of certain times in his life. He hoped they would jog his memory in his later years. In the box from that year was an assortment of mementos. He noticed a coaster he had kept from the restaurant he would often have lunch at. Many of the other employees at Magnus' company would meet at the restaurant for lunch or drinks. He smiled a little as he recalled how often the conversation was centered on Magnus' lack of personality. He didn't make friends easily. Walt understood that. He didn't make friends easily either. In fact most of the conversations he overheard were as a result of no one noticing that he was there.

"Four months." He nodded. "I was only there for four months. It wasn't a full year contract." He began to dig through more of the papers in the box. He could remember what he did for Magnus, but maybe he had forgotten some details. He had written down exactly what he had done and even kept a copy of the contract. During that time in his life he had tried to generate as much money as he could and took on far more jobs than he should have. Magnus' company was one of those. He did it more for the connections it would afford him than for the money, as Magnus wasn't the most generous person.

The more Walt searched the more memories returned to him. He recalled holding the offer in his hand. It was delivered by a messenger direct to his door, which impressed him. But when he saw who it was from he hesitated. Magnus' reputation for being vicious made him think twice about working with him. Yet the benefit outweighed the discomfort.

Walt always made the logical choice. As he sat back and stared into the box his mind reeled. He wished that just that once he'd gone with his instincts rather than the logical choice. He spent the remainder of the night elbow deep in the box. Every scrap of paper that might provide some insight he settled into a separate pile. However, even as the clock struck one in the morning, he had very little to go on. He closed his eyes for a moment as a wave of exhaustion washed over him. When he opened them again he looked into the empty space in front of him.

"Why Magnus? Why me?"

His words vanished into thin air. There was no one to answer his question. The idea that the question might never be answered launched Walt right back into a state of unease. Walt did his very best to avoid unanswerable questions, such as the meaning of life, and what happened after death. He preferred to debate on topics that had set and solid answers. The idea of never being able to come to a conclusion made him break out in a sweat. He took a deep breath and continued to sort through the papers. There had to be an answer. He wasn't sure if he would be able to survive without one.

Chapter Four

Early the next morning Eddy pulled up in front of Samantha's villa. As she had promised she would be, she was ready to go. When she opened the passenger door of the car the scent of coffee filled the vehicle. She offered him a cup.

"Just brewed."

"Maybe just a little. Thanks." He took the cup and put it in the cup holder in the middle console. He gripped it so tight that his hand shook in the process.

"What's wrong?" Samantha raised an eyebrow.

"I'm worried about Walt."

"You said the alibi would clear him."

"It does, mostly. But that's not what I'm worried about. You know how he is, he's going to obsess over this. Whether or not he's a suspect he's going to want to know who did it, just like we

43

would. He called me just after sunrise this morning. I don't think he slept."

"Did he think of anything that might be relevant?" Samantha asked.

"Only that he can recall a few things about working for Magnus, but nothing personal. No reason why he would have written down his name."

"It must be driving him insane." Samantha sighed and looked out through the windshield. "You're right." She sat back against the car seat as Eddy took off down the road. "He's not going to let it go no matter what. So, we just have to solve it." She shrugged. "It's as simple as that."

"I wish it was really that simple. But these high profile cases are never that simple. You know that."

"Maybe this one will be. Sometimes you just have to have a positive attitude."

"You're the only person I know that can find the silver lining in murder."

"It's not finding the silver lining, Eddy, it's not admitting defeat before you've attempted the battle." She tilted her head to the side as she looked at him. "You seem more apprehensive than usual? What's going on under that hat?"

"I want to be positive about this, Samantha, but I also don't want to miss anything. One wrong move and Walt could end up in jail. That's bad enough for anyone, but for Walt it would be his worst nightmare."

Samantha rested her hand on the back of his. She met his eyes with a gentle smile. "You're not responsible for this, Eddy. Yes, we need to do everything we can, but the chips are going to fall, and you're not going to be able to control where they fall, no matter how much you want to."

Eddy cringed and eased the car to a stop at a red light. "So you say, but I'm the one with police experience. I know that the detectives are gunning for Walt. I know that the more nervous Walt gets the guiltier he will look."

"Then it's a good thing he has you to look out for him, Eddy. Just remember, we have to take things one step at a time. Let's find out exactly what happened first, then we'll figure out how to best protect Walt. All right?"

"All right." He nodded and turned down another road that led to Magnus' company. "I wonder if we will even be able to get inside."

"Leave that to me." Samantha smiled with confidence. Eddy glanced over at her and couldn't help but smile back. Samantha had that aura of determination that always made him certain she could accomplish anything she put her mind to.

After a few more minutes of travel Eddy slowed down in front of a building. He checked the address, then turned into the nearly empty parking lot.

The building itself was fairly small, square, and paneled with glass windows. Samantha studied it with a hint of surprise.

"What's on your mind?" Eddy looked over at

her.

"I don't know. I guess I just expected it to be bigger."

"Not quite as intimidating in reality as it was on paper, hm?"

Samantha nodded slowly, still fascinated by what she saw. "I have a feeling that will change once we go inside."

"Maybe." Eddy gripped the steering wheel and parked the car. "But in my experience the bigger the bluster the weaker the bite."

Samantha narrowed her eyes as she spotted a security guard step out of the building. "It looks like there's a card reader to get in the door, we have to hurry so I can get the security guard to let us in."

"How? Never mind." He shook his head and climbed out of the car. He followed right behind her as she hurried up to the security guard.

"Excuse me, Sir?"

He paused and looked at her. "Yes?"

"Are you Matthew?"

"Matthew?" He raised an eyebrow. "No."

"Are you sure?" Samantha sighed.

"Uh, yes, I'm sure. My name is Chuck."

"Oh darn, I must have gotten the names mixed up. This is terrible. I was supposed to be issued a security card to get inside, but I'm running late, and I've left my paperwork at home." Her voice shook as she spoke. "Everything that could go wrong has gone wrong today."

"Ma'am, the building is closed, why would you need to get inside?"

"Because I was here yesterday. I had a meeting with Mr. Magnus, and we got into it, you know."

"Oh, I know." Chuck laughed. "He wasn't easy to get along with."

"Well, I guess in my haste I left my phone inside. It has all of my pictures on it of my grandkids, and my cats." She blinked back tears. "They are the only photos I have and if I lose the phone I will have no pictures of my grandkids growing up or of Boots as a kitten."

"Calm down, just calm down." He frowned and looked past her at Eddy. Eddy did his best to look upset.

"Please Sir, my wife here, she's lost without her phone. She knows it's inside, she just needs to grab it."

"I wasn't informed about any lost phone." He frowned and pulled out a small notebook. "No one let me know that anyone was coming in."

"Maybe they forgot. With what happened last night." Eddy lowered his voice. "Such a horrible act."

"Oh yes, I can see how messages might have gotten lost."

"I'm so worried that my phone might get lost in the investigation. I'll just be a minute..."

"I'm going off shift soon. I'll let you in, but

you're going to have to find your way out. There's only one person in there today anyway and he's in his office so I don't see what harm it could do."

"No harm at all, I promise." Samantha wiped at her eyes. "Oh, you're such a good man, such an angel, you've really saved me."

"Just don't mention my name if you get caught, all right?" He smiled a little and walked back to the door of the building. He ran his keycard through the scanner and the door lock retracted.

"Thank you, so much."

"Hey, I have cats, too." He patted her shoulder. "They're so cute when they're kittens."

Samantha and Eddy stepped inside before Chuck could change his mind.

"Laying it on a little thick weren't you?" Eddy quirked an eyebrow.

"Hey, cats and kids will get them every time. It doesn't hurt that I look so harmless."

"If only the world knew the truth." He nudged her with his elbow.

"Hush." Samantha grinned. The long front hall was devoid of any other people. Samantha noticed that as the security guard had said every office they passed was empty. "They probably shut down the building for the investigation." She frowned as she rounded a slight curve in the hall.

"I would think they would take a couple of days to get a handle on the loss," Eddy said.

"Still, a place like this won't stay closed long."

"There's the main office." Eddy pointed out an office that looked a lot like the exterior of the building. It was square with walls formed from glass. Though there were blinds to cover the windows when desired, they were not lowered. Both Eddy and Samantha had a clear view of the man who sat inside the office at a large, maple desk. His back was to them as he stared at a computer monitor. "What do you think?" Eddy leaned closer to her. "Can we get past him?"

"Maybe, but I don't think we should. I think we should talk to him."

"He might throw us right out."

"He might, but I don't know that he'd go to all of that trouble. Besides, I have an idea. Just follow my lead."

"It's worked so far."

Samantha took the lead and knocked lightly on the door. The man inside either didn't hear her or chose to ignore her. When she knocked again, he turned in his chair. He stared through the glass at her for a long moment. The grimace on his face indicated he wasn't pleased to be interrupted. Samantha forced a smile to her lips. He stood up from the chair and walked towards the door. When he opened it she found that he was even less pleased.

"Do you have a reason to be here?"

"Yes, actually I do. I thought you might be able to answer a few questions for me."

"Questions about what?" He stood in the

doorway which blocked Samantha and Eddy.

"Lawrence Magnus." Samantha managed another smile. "He hired me."

"Hired you?"

"Well us. Well, he hired me, and then I hired Eddy here. He's a retired detective."

"Wait a minute, what are you talking about? What did he hire you for?"

"You know how concerned he was about his safety. He had me on retainer. In the event of an untimely death he wanted an independent investigation into what happened to him. Unfortunately he is gone, and now I am here. I hired my own detective." She smiled at Eddy. "Best in the business."

"That sounds like something you should discuss with his lawyer."

"Oh, I will, just as soon as I have the opportunity to assess the crime scene. Obviously, I take my job very seriously. I can't trust just anyone, now can I? If I don't get a chance to look

53

at the crime scene right away then you can expect a lawsuit to be filed against you by the end of business today. I have the contract signed, but if I have to take the time to produce the paperwork I will move forward with a lawsuit."

The man rolled his eyes and opened the door wider for them. "What does it matter? He's dead anyway."

"It was important to him." Samantha frowned as she stepped through the door. "Maybe he didn't think that anyone would care to investigate his death properly. Who might I ask, are you?"

"I'm Jimmy Barker. I'm acting in charge until a new CEO is appointed."

"Magnus must have trusted you then." Eddy stepped in behind Samantha and closed the door.

"Magnus didn't trust anyone." Jimmy narrowed his eyes. "He appointed me because he knew that I would have too much loyalty to just walk away. Although, I wish he hadn't with this mess he left behind."

"Mess?" Samantha tried to peer over his shoulder at the computer screen. "Was there some kind of problem?"

"If there was it's hard to tell now. Whoever tried to access the computer files triggered a security response. Files have been deleting all night. I can barely figure out what is left. I don't have any clue how I am going to explain this to the board. It's as if twenty years of work is completely wiped out." He ran his hands back through his hair and groaned. "I know the man is dead, but the last thing I want is to be in charge of all of this."

"Maybe I could take a look. I know a little bit about computers," Samantha said.

"No, thank you." He locked eyes with her. "I know a thing or two about people who want to be nosy, and you're coming across very nosy. If I wanted you involved in this I would ask."

"All right, take a breath there. She's only

trying to help." Eddy stepped closer to Samantha. "Now, about the crime scene?"

"It's right over there." He pointed through the glass wall of the office towards an area filled with cubicles. Samantha could see a yellow police line near the hallway. Eddy nodded and opened the door for her.

"Let's go have a look," Eddy said.

"Sure, just don't touch the tape." Jimmy turned back to the computer and struck the keys with sharp deliberate movements.

"Jimmy, just one quick question." Samantha paused in the doorway.

"What is it?" Jimmy sighed and refused to look back at her.

"Who found Magnus?"

"Oh, the night shift employee."

"He didn't see who did it?" Samantha asked.

Jimmy turned in his chair to look at her. "It's a bit difficult to see when you're knocked out cold, don't you think?"

"He was knocked out before the murder?"

"Yes."

"Was there anyone else working at the time?"

"No. Any other questions you should probably direct to Detective Jenson."

Eddy winced at the mention of the man. If it got back to Detective Jenson that they were allowed to see the crime scene, things could get ugly quick.

"Thanks, we already spoke with him. We'll be sure to keep in contact with him," Samantha replied.

"Good." Jimmy nodded and turned back to his computer. Samantha and Eddy made their way down the hall to the area of the crime scene. Yellow police tape surrounded an overturned chair and a few crime scene markers on the floor. Eddy took a few steps back so that he could see the entire crime scene. Samantha zeroed in on the overturned chair.

"It looks like the intruder was surprised by Magnus."

"Maybe if he was sitting at this computer then he might have jumped up fast enough to knock the chair over. But I think it is more likely that it was knocked over when he attacked Magnus because he was hit over the head from behind," Eddy said.

"Maybe the intruder saw Magnus enter the building and then approached him from behind," Samantha suggested.

Eddy tilted his head to the side and looked over the path between the overturned chair and where he stood. "Did Magnus know that the intruder was here? Or did he just happen to take this path? Is there somewhere else Magnus could have been heading?"

Samantha looked towards a sign that hung above the next hallway. "Restroom."

"Wouldn't he have a private one though?"

"Maybe, but when you have to go you have to go. Maybe this one was the closest. Or maybe he felt comfortable using it since just about everyone else was out of the office."

"Yes, that's possible."

"Maybe the murderer saw Magnus on the way to the restroom and panicked and hit him," Samantha suggested.

"It must have been someone who had a lot to lose if they were caught." Eddy squinted at the space on the desk where the computer should have been. "I suppose the police techs are running scans on the computer right this second. They'll likely be able to pinpoint more information from what they find."

"What if the intruder wasn't just here to get into the computer? What if he was here to kill Magnus from the beginning?"

"Premeditated?" Eddy looked up at her. "It's something to consider." He stood up and glanced over his shoulder in the direction of the main office. "We shouldn't stay too long. Jimmy might get suspicious and I'm sure the new security guard will be on shift in a few minutes."

"There's not much more for us to see here. Let's head back and check in with Walt. He's probably desperate for an update."

"You're right."

Samantha turned and took one last look around, then she snapped a picture with her cell phone.

"There is one thing I'm curious about." Eddy frowned as he fell into step beside her. "How did the intruder get in without a keycard?"

"That's a good question." Samantha slid her phone into her purse. "I think we should ask Jimmy about it on the way out."

"I don't think we're going to find out much more from Jimmy. He wasn't exactly very talkative, or friendly." Eddy paused beside the glass office.

"Maybe not, but I am very good at getting people to talk." Samantha smiled. She peeked into the office and saw that Jimmy was on the telephone. She leaned close to the glass. "It's too thick, I can't hear anything."

"Maybe if we get inside, we'll get an idea of who he is talking to."

Samantha nodded and grabbed the handle of the door. She didn't knock, she just pushed the door open and stepped inside. Jimmy shifted in his chair to look at her with the telephone still pressed against his ear. He glared but then turned away again.

"I'm doing everything that I can. You have no idea what I am dealing with. I'll have to call you back later." He pulled the phone from his ear and set it on the desk beside him. As he turned to look at Samantha she tried to get a glimpse of the screen of the phone, but Jimmy's elbow blocked it. "What is it?"

"I was just wondering if you could tell me about Magnus' normal schedule. Would he usually be here so late?" Samantha asked.

"He kept odd hours, he would come and go as

he pleased, but I guess I would say that it was a little on the later side for him to come in. What does that matter?"

"Maybe he came in at that time for a reason. That might give us a clue as to the motive of the murderer," Samantha said.

"The motive was that the guy got caught doing something he shouldn't have been doing. That could be motive enough don't you think?" Jimmy grimaced.

Samantha gripped the strap of her purse and looked into his eyes. "Do you think there was some problem that he came in to deal with? Maybe someone called or sent him an e-mail?"

Jimmy chuckled and shook his head. "No, if there was he would have just called me, I was always the one to handle any issues, especially after hours. Magnus only ever did things that benefited him."

"Maybe that had something to do with it?" Samantha leaned a little closer to him. "Maybe he had his hands into something less than legal?"

"Not a chance." Jimmy locked his eyes to hers. "Magnus was a lot of things, but stupid wasn't one of them. He wouldn't risk losing the entire company and his fortune over a few broken laws."

"Thank you for your time." Samantha nodded.

"You didn't exactly give me a choice." Jimmy turned back to the computer. As Samantha stepped out of the office Eddy held the door for her. They walked quickly towards the exit. They didn't exchange a word until they were out of the building.

"So, what do you think?" Eddy lifted an eyebrow.

"I think that Jimmy is hiding something. I also think that Magnus had a few secrets."

"I agree."

As they walked back towards the car Samantha tapped her fingertips against the side of her purse. The repetitive sound drew Eddy's attention. He glanced over at her in the same moment that he opened the car door for her.

"What is it? I know that look," Eddy said.

"I don't know. Everything seems too simple."

"Simple?" Eddy walked around to the driver's side and settled into his seat. Then he looked over at her for an explanation.

"Magnus just happens to walk in as an intruder is sifting through the computer?" Samantha shook her head. "It seems like an impossible coincidence."

Eddy started the car. "You think that Magnus might have known there was an intruder?"

"Maybe. Why else would he come in at such an odd hour? Maybe something or someone tipped him off to the person's presence there," Samantha said.

"Interesting. We'll have to look into the security systems that are in place."

"He might have had a private security system

of some kind. If he was the paranoid type."

"Seems to me that he had reason to be paranoid," Eddy said.

"Well, if he didn't have much in the way of family, then his employees, the people he worked with every day are going to be our best resource," Samantha said.

"I agree."

"I'll see if I can get a list of all of the employees that work for the company. From there we can narrow down who might have had access to the building during the time of the murder."

"Good idea. I'll see what I can find out about the crime scene, and whether any witnesses have been found," Eddy said.

"Good thinking."

"Sometimes I wonder if wealth only leads to these kinds of problems. I used to be a little bitter about not doing more with my life, but when these types of things happen, I'm glad all I have is my old chair and my little villa."

"That seems like a lot to me." Samantha smiled wistfully as she looked out through the car window. "There was a time when I didn't have a place to call home. I was moving between hotels chasing stories. I love my little villa. And the friends that I've made."

Eddy glanced over at her and smiled. "It is nice to have each other to turn to. Especially at times like this. I just hope that our friendship will be enough."

"We'll get Walt through this, I have no doubt in my mind."

"That's what I respect about you, Samantha. I give you a hard time about your optimism, but your confidence is so unwavering. It makes me think that there might still be good things in the world."

"You're not really that jaded are you, Eddy? There must be some things that still inspire you."

He gripped the steering wheel so tight that his knuckles grew white. After a moment of silence he looked over at her again.

"I still get inspired by trying to make sure that justice is served."

"Well, that's important," Samantha said.

"Call me with anything you find. I'll talk to Walt. We should all get together and discuss this when we have a little more information."

"Okay, I'll drum up every connection I can find at the company, and I'll also look into Magnus' personal connections."

"Okay, I'll see if Chris can give me any more information." Eddy nodded.

Samantha stepped out of the car and waved to Eddy as he pulled away.

Chapter Five

Samantha unlocked the door to her villa with her thoughts spinning. Time mattered in this situation. If she didn't find something fast then the focus could easily remain on Walt. She settled in front of her computer and navigated her way into the company's website. On the surface it was a simple site designed for large clients. She tried to find her way into the system to access the employee files, but they were highly protected.

"Dead end." She frowned as her phone beeped. It was a text from Eddy with a picture attached.

Couldn't get employee list yet but this is from the company files. I thought it might be helpful.

Samantha decided to print out the list. She looked at the list which was of four digit numbers.

She looked through it but couldn't see the number 6886 on it. Another dead end.

After a deep breath she refocused. Maybe the list from Eddy and the website couldn't provide her with what she needed, but there were other ways to get the information. She conducted several searches on different social media sites with the name of the company. After a few dead ends she came up with several posts about a baseball team made up of company employees. That gave her several names. Those names allowed her to search individual social media sites, which allowed her to find several more names connected to those that listed their workplace as the company. By the time she was done she had over one hundred names. From her research it appeared that some of the people on the baseball team no longer worked at the company, but she kept them on the list in case they could provide some information.

It was easy to discover just how Magnus' employees felt about him as well. There were several posts about his merit as a boss, and none were flattering, though she didn't notice any that went to the extreme of implying a threat. However, there might have been some she missed. With the new list she began to search each individual to find contact information. By the time she was done she had a nice list to work from. It would give them a lot to discuss at the meeting. She picked up her phone and dialed Jo.

"Hi Jo. Just wanted to update you. We went to the company this morning, but didn't find too much to go on. I've got a pretty thorough list of employees though."

"That's a good place to start. Many people want to murder their bosses."

"I think most are just joking." Samantha raised an eyebrow. "At least I hope so."

"Maybe, but you never know. I wouldn't be surprised if whoever murdered Magnus is on that list."

"Maybe." Samantha sighed and looked over

the list again. "But it's a very long list, and we don't have a very long time."

"Divide and conquer, it works every time." Jo's voice lightened. "I'm sure that we can all do our share."

"That's a good plan. I have to tell you that Eddy and I are both pretty worried about Walt."

"Well, that makes three of us. I'm pretty worried, too. When are we meeting?"

"At three."

"Okay, I'll be there."

"Thanks Jo." Samantha hung up the phone and picked up her list of names. As she counted up the names she noticed the piece of paper with the four digit codes on it. It seemed to her that there were about the same amount of codes as there were names. Maybe the codes identified the employees? She paper clipped the two lists together to investigate it later.

Samantha made herself a small lunch and set a notepad on the table beside her. She often found that she came up with the best ideas when she wasn't looking for an idea. As she enjoyed her sandwich her mind slowly went over the events of the morning. Jimmy, annoyed at being thrust into his position, and not the least bit hurt by his boss' demise. That was enough to make her suspicious of him. Even if someone didn't like their boss, they would likely feel something about his death. Did Jimmy's lack of concern make him a sociopath? Or was it psychopath? Or was he just grieving in his own way?

Samantha sighed and took another bite of her sandwich. As she chewed the lists of names and numbers flashed through her thoughts. If each of those codes was assigned to each of the employees that might mean that there would be a way to tell who entered and exited the building around the time of the murder. That would certainly narrow down the suspect list. That's presuming they used the front entrance, but maybe they broke in or there was another way to access the building without breaking in. She finished her sandwich then picked up the phone to call Eddy. He answered around a mouthful of his lunch.

"Hello?"

"Hi Eddy, sorry I caught you in the middle of lunch."

"It's all right. Did you find something?"

"I came across a good amount of information about the employees. I think the list of four digit numbers might correlate to each of the employees. I was wondering if your police contact that sent it to you had any information about that. Maybe the police spoke to Jimmy and found out whether that four digit number is a code or not. Maybe it was connected to the keycard the murderer used to get inside. If that's the case we might be able to narrow down our suspect list. What do you think?"

"I think you're brilliant as always, Samantha. I'll check into it right now. I wanted to get an update on the case before I talk to Walt anyway. We're still meeting at three right?"

"Yes, and Jo is eager to pitch in."

"Great, we're going to need all of our guns on this one." When he hung up the phone Eddy picked up the last of his grilled cheese sandwich. It was a bit too greasy for his liking, a result of his distracted mind. He took the last bite then dialed Chris' number. After three rings he answered.

"Hello?"

"Chris, it's Eddy."

"Oh, Eddy I was just about to call you."

"Yes?"

"I've got an update for you."

"Great. What is it?"

"Firstly, it doesn't look like the building was broken into in anyway so it is likely that the murderer accessed the building through the front door."

"Interesting," Eddy said. "And secondly."

"It's good news. They have another suspect."

"Oh great, who is it?"

"Jimmy."

"Wait, Jimmy Barker?"

"Yes, that's him."

"Wow, we just talked with him this morning."

"You did? How?"

"Samantha and I went to the company to check out the crime scene."

"You are bold, you know that?"

"I try not to disappoint."

"What if you had been caught?"

"Don't worry. I would never turn you in, Chris."

"Did you ever consider that I might not be as worried about that, as I am about you ending up behind bars? At your age?"

"At my age?" Eddy snapped. "I'll have you know, at my age, I'm still perfectly capable of handling myself behind bars."

"I didn't mean any offense." Chris sighed.

"Just be cautious."

"I intend to be. Now, what is this about Jimmy being a suspect?"

"It turns out surveillance cameras caught him entering the building around seven in the evening."

"Okay, but that's before the estimated time of death."

"Yes, and he's seen leaving about fifteen minutes later. Then an hour later he is seen entering the building again."

"Well, that should do it shouldn't it?"

"It should, except as of now he has an alibi."

"How can he if he's on camera?"

"A man in a baseball cap is on camera. His face isn't visible. Jimmy belongs to a baseball team and he and his teammates were at a dinner during the time frame of the murder. He says he lost his keycard some time after he visited the building, but he can't pinpoint the exact time and he said he didn't enter the building a second time. It's a convenient story, but because of the alibi we need to establish that the alibi is false in order to make him a viable suspect."

"Yikes, that doesn't make him a great suspect."

"No it doesn't, but it's something."

"Walt has a good alibi, too, so maybe there will be less attention on him."

"Maybe."

"Can you see if you can get a list of Jimmy's financial transactions so we can see if there are any discrepancies?" Eddy asked.

"I'll try."

"Thank you. Did you find out anything else?"

"It looks like that financial software was the only part of the program targeted. It handles the billing and collections."

"So, he was trying to transfer funds?"

"I don't think so actually. We're still trying to

get a good grasp on the system, but it appears to be more about checks and balances than actual funds. Maybe it was a first step before he tried to crack into the bank account information."

"Interesting. I have a question for you."

"Sure."

"That four digit code list, did you find out any more information about it?" Eddy asked.

"Yes actually. The four digit code represents an employee's ID number. However, that code in particular is not currently associated with anyone at the company."

"What about the keycards, do they use the same four digit code?"

"Yes, they do. But again, the code itself isn't associated with anyone."

"But you should be able to tell by the numbers who entered the building through the front door around the time of the murder?"

"Yes. At least I think so," Chris said.

"Is there any way you can get me a copy of who entered the building and the surveillance video?"

"Hm. I can try. This is pretty high profile so I have to watch my step. If I manage to get it, I'll get it to you as soon as I can."

"Thanks Chris."

"You're welcome. Next time you do something risky like going to the scene of a crime how about if you tell me first? That way I can at least have your back."

"That's why I don't tell you, Chris. You do enough as it is. I won't have you taking more risks for me. Okay?"

"You don't have to worry about me, Eddy." He hung up before Eddy could argue. Not that there would be much of an argument. Chris always did whatever he pleased. As soon as Eddy hung up he dialed Walt's number.

Walt picked up the phone on the first ring.

"Yes? What is it? Did you find something?"

"Walt, are you okay?" The high-pitched tone of Walt's voice surprised Eddy.

"I might have had too much coffee."

"I can tell, Bud." Eddy shook his head. "Listen, there is another suspect, the acting CEO, Jimmy Barker."

"Oh wonderful." Walt sighed with relief. "Did he do it?"

"We're not sure yet. It looks like he has an alibi."

"Then how can he be a suspect?"

"It's complicated, but his keycard, which he claims was stolen, was used to access the building around the time of the murder. The person, that we believe is Jimmy, was caught on surveillance wearing a baseball cap when he entered the building earlier as well as around the time of the murder, so I'm guessing he might have found a way to fake his alibi. There's something else, too."

"What is it?"

"The software that was accessed was a financial program that handled the billing and collections for the company. It made me think of you."

"You're kidding!" Walt's voice grew even higher. "Unless he updated the program over the years, that is likely the same system I installed for him."

"Maybe that has something to do with why he wrote down your name on the piece of paper."

"Maybe it does. Maybe." Walt sighed. "But this doesn't improve my situation does it? Now, not only did Magnus write down my name, but presuming it hasn't been changed the software accessed was installed and customized by me."

"It doesn't mean too much, other than, you might be able to figure out why the intruder was in that software. What could he have been looking for?"

"I'm not sure what would benefit him. Maybe the details of the contracted company's payment methods? Even that would be a stretch, as most have enough protection on them that any false charges would be flagged right away."

"Anything else then? Maybe a way to filter money between accounts?"

"No, it's nothing like that. The program doesn't provide access to any actual funds. It's mainly for record keeping."

"Odd. Maybe they went into the wrong program?" Eddy suggested.

"Maybe. If I could take a look at that computer I might be able to figure out more."

"I don't think that's an option."

"Yes, I guess not."

"Maybe you can do the next best thing."

"What do you mean?"

"Can you recreate the software on your computer?"

"I think that I could."

"If you did, you could experiment to see what

the intruder might have been after."

"That's a brilliant idea, Eddy. Thank you."

"You work on that, and I'll work on a few other things. Don't forget we're meeting up with Samantha and Jo at three."

"Yes. I hate to cause everyone so much trouble."

"Walt, we are sorry you're in this position, but we're glad to be able to help. Besides this isn't just about you. It's about a murder that needs to be solved. Clearing your name in the process is just a bonus."

"That's true."

Chapter Six

After hanging up the phone with Walt, Eddy tried to focus on the case. The best way to figure it out was with the help of Samantha, Jo and Walt. He took some time to clean up after himself then settled in his easy chair. There was just enough time for a nap which he seemed to be needing more and more lately. As he was about to fall asleep, someone knocked on the door. He bolted up out of his chair, half-awake and prepared to defend himself if he needed to. A consequence of working so many years as a police officer, was his jumpy nature. He walked over to the door and opened it to find Jo outside. She wore her long, dark hair in a tight ponytail. Her lips tightened at the sight of him.

"Can I come in?"

"Uh, sure. I thought we were meeting at three." He stepped aside. She moved past him and tilted her head towards the door.

"Close it."

"Okay." Eddy stared at her as he closed the door. "What's going on?"

"I'm not sure if there's a good way to say this, so I'm just going to say it. How well do you know Walt?"

"I know him pretty well. Why?"

"Before I go all out on this investigation, I want to know that he wasn't involved." She folded her arms across her chest.

"Jo, that's crazy. Walt would never hurt anyone."

"Maybe." She shrugged. "But something I turned up makes me wonder."

"What's that?'

"Did Walt tell you that he was fired from Magnus' company?" She raised an eyebrow.

"No." Eddy's jaw clenched and he shook his head. "I'm sure if that were true he would have told me."

"I have sources of my own."

"I know all about your sources." Eddy rolled his eyes. He had tried to put Jo's past career as a cat burglar behind him, but it was often on his mind.

"Whatever." Jo shrugged. "If you don't want to know then I won't bother to tell you. Walt has supported me on more than one occasion and I came to you first because I know what good friends you and Walt are." She started to walk towards the door.

"Wait a minute." Eddy stepped between her and the door. "Tell me what you know."

"Why should I?" She stared into his eyes. "You wouldn't believe me anyway."

"I do." He sighed and lowered his voice. "I do, Jo, you should know that. I'm sorry for the comment."

"You should be. I thought we were over the suspicion," Jo said.

"Really?" He laughed a little. "You're telling

me that we're past the suspicion, but here you are questioning Walt's integrity. So am I supposed to trust you, if you don't trust us?"

"You are not Walt." She narrowed her eyes. "I came to you didn't I?"

"Yes." His shoulders relaxed. "Yes, you did. So what did you hear?"

"Well, when Samantha mentioned Magnus' name I thought it sounded familiar. So I looked into it. Turns out this man has made more than a few enemies, especially in the criminal world. In fact, there's a bounty on his head and it's only one of the many over the years."

"Why wouldn't the police know about this?"

"Magnus has remained squeaky clean. No arrests, no suspicions. No reason to dig into his life or the people that might hate him."

"That makes sense. But why do you suspect Walt?"

"I didn't say I did. When I asked if there were any people that stood out as enemies to Magnus my source told me that the reason Walt was fired was because he was going to turn Magnus in for something unsavory. That gives him motive, revenge."

"Walt isn't the vengeful type. He also isn't the type to let something go if he knew it was illegal."

"According to what I was told, Walt backed off when Magnus threatened him. Maybe he has held this over Walt's head for all these years. Magnus was manipulative."

"That seems impossible. It's been so many years. Besides, it's Walt we're talking about." He narrowed his eyes. "He wouldn't keep something like that a secret."

"Then why didn't he tell you about being fired? Did he even tell you why he thought about turning in Magnus?"

Eddy lowered his eyes. "No, he didn't tell me anything about that."

"See? There might be a reason."

"I doubt that."

"Doubt it all you want but we need to have a plan in case it's the truth."

"What do you mean a plan?" He took a step away from the door.

"Well, if he took care of the problem, or was involved in some way, we need to be prepared to protect him. Get him out of the country, or something." Jo shrugged.

"Are you serious?" Eddy's jaw rippled.

"Of course I am. These things go much smoother when you plan ahead."

"If Walt was involved, which I'm sure he wasn't, I wouldn't do anything to protect him. I'd turn him into the police myself."

Jo's face paled at his words. "Even after everything he's done for you?"

"He's a friend, Jo, but murder is murder."

"And you wonder why people don't trust you?" Jo shook her head. "I wish I'd never told you."

"People do trust me, Jo. Because I stand for justice. Even if that means that a friend has to pay the price. Don't even think of questioning my friendship with Walt. Because you're the one who is ready to protect him from a crime he didn't commit, and I am the one who knows with unwavering certainty that he did not commit that crime. I will protect him from false accusations, because I trust him. Maybe you should consider that option instead of looking up which countries don't extradite."

Jo frowned and moved past him towards the door. "Never mind. I shouldn't have come here."

"Wait." Eddy placed a hand on the door to prevent her from opening it. "The information is good, Jo. It could help us figure out all of this. But I can tell you right now, if you accuse Walt of anything, he's not going to forgive you for it. He's an honorable man."

"Wouldn't be right for someone like me to accuse someone like him right?" She peered at him through a few stray wisps of hair that had escaped her ponytail. "Since he's so honorable?"

Eddy sighed and straightened up. "That's not what I meant. Your opinion matters to him, it matters to us all, and it would hurt him to think that you might consider him capable of murder."

"Isn't everyone capable?" She tilted her head to the side. "Given the right circumstances anyone can be pushed that far."

"I don't think so. Not everyone."

"You?"

"Me. You?" He quirked an eyebrow.

"Definitely."

"But not Walt." He looked into her eyes. "I promise you, not Walt."

"Then I'll leave this information with you, Eddy. You can decide what you want to do with it. But don't tell me I didn't warn you." She brushed his hand away from the door and opened it. "I hope that you'll have that same faith in me one day."

Eddy could only nod. His trust in Jo certainly increased the more he got to know her, but she did have a criminal past. Walt did not. As soon as Jo left, Eddy grabbed his keys and wallet. He headed out to Walt's villa.

Chapter Seven

Walt's legs ached from pacing. He sat back down in front of the computer. It was fairly simple for him to recreate the program he'd designed for Magnus. However, there was no way to be sure that it was the same one that the company still used. The more he manipulated the data, the more he narrowed down the motive of whoever might have been using it. There was only one benefit he could see from hacking into the program. That was to erase debt. The company relied on the system to generate bills, current, and past due invoices. If a person's debt was removed from the system no bills would be generated, and there would be no paper trail of proof of debt. It would essentially vanish. However, it was a huge jump to go from erasing debt to murder.

Walt's mind still swirled with anxiety over the phone call in the first place. He had to get control of his thoughts before the meeting. He didn't want any information to slip out by accident. His personal business was his, no one else's. He went through the program again, in the role of an intruder. What did he want from the program? What changes could he make that would benefit him? Again, he found that the only benefit was the potential for wiping out debt. He sat back in his chair and sighed. Even though the case centered around him it seemed that there wasn't much he could do to help with the investigation. He glanced at his watch. Still a half hour before the meeting. With a yawn he stood up and stretched. As he lowered his arms there was a knock at the door. He turned and strode towards the door. When he opened it, Eddy stood on the other side.

"You're early, Eddy. Did you find out something new?"

Eddy dipped his hat down along his forehead some. "You could say that." He locked eyes with Walt. Walt's heart skipped a beat. Eddy could be quite intimidating when he wanted to be.

"What is it?"

"We should talk inside." He stepped past Walt into the villa. Walt closed the door and braced himself for what might come next. Were the police on their way? Did they find more evidence against him?

"Walt, you know that we're friends, right?" Eddy looked over at him.

"Sure, of course I do. What's this about?"

"If we're going to investigate this murder, we really need all of the information. Everything that might be relevant."

Walt leaned back against the door of the villa and nodded. "I know that."

"So. Is there anything you might want to share with me?"

"Don't you have secrets, Eddy?" Walt raised an eyebrow. "I don't know every little thing there is to know about you."

"No, you certainly don't. But I'm not the one who needs to provide information here."

"Look, I don't want to talk about it. It has nothing to do with the case."

"It's going to come up in the police investigation, you know that right? When it does, you're going to look even more suspicious."

Walt swallowed hard. "I hoped it would be solved before it got to that."

"So, it's true?" Eddy sighed. "Walt, why won't you tell me?"

"Eddy, it's not as simple as just telling you. It's something I've tried to forget about for many years." Walt shook his head. "If I thought it pertained to the case, I would have told you."

"Maybe it's not your place to decide that, Walt. I know you value your privacy, but we're all putting our necks on the line by looking into this. Magnus was a powerful man. You don't need to be ashamed."

"Ashamed?" Walt looked up at him with surprise. "I'm not ashamed at all."

"Not for staying silent?"

"Staying silent?" Walt shook his head. "I think someone gave you the wrong information."

"So maybe you should give me the right information?"

"Maybe it's best if I tell everyone at once. I'm sure you didn't come by this information on your own. If I'm going to tell you, I might as well tell everyone. But first, who told you?" Walt stepped away from the door and closer to Eddy. "Samantha?"

"No." Eddy cleared his throat. "It was Jo. A contact in the criminal world gave her the information."

"That explains why it's a little slanted. So why are you here and not her? She didn't think she could come to me with this information?"

"I asked her not to." Eddy shoved his hands in his pockets.

"Why?"

"I didn't want you to think that she didn't trust you."

"Jo?" He laughed. "Jo doesn't trust anyone. That's just her nature. Was she ready to turn me in or something?"

"Quite the opposite." Eddy smiled. "She was planning your getaway."

Walt smiled, too. "That's the Jo I know. At least she has my back."

"I do too, Walt. I just need to know what is going on, so that I know how to look out for you."

"I wish none of you had to even think about looking out for me, Eddy. This was a mess when I worked for Magnus, and it's a mess now. But it's nothing that you're thinking. I didn't do anything wrong, and I didn't keep my silence. In fact, not keeping my silence is what I regret."

"Why is that?"

"Let's just say Magnus was powerful then, too. After working with him, and doing what I did, I didn't get very much business."

"He trashed your name?"

"Essentially. Like I said, we should wait."

"It's about time now. Let's head over to Samantha's."

"Eddy, it's not what you think." Walt met his eyes.

"What I think is that you should have told me this from the beginning, Walt." Eddy frowned.

"You're right, I probably should have."

"From now on, no hiding things, all right?" Eddy opened the door for him.

"All right." Walt nodded. As Walt stepped through the door Eddy's phone beeped. He looked at it to see it was a text from Chris.

Envelope in mailbox

"I need to pick up a letter on the way," Eddy said as he walked with Walt to the mailbox. He scanned his surroundings as he opened the mailbox. Then he reached in and took out the

99

envelope. He took the papers out and looked at the front page then put it back in the envelope. "This is a list of Jimmy's transactions from his account."

"That was quick."

"Will you be able to look at them and see if you find anything suspicious?" Eddy asked as he handed the envelope to Walt.

"Yes, of course," Walt said as they continued towards Samantha's villa. "Hopefully there will be a payment to a trained assassin in here."

Eddy smiled.

Chapter Eight

Samantha eagerly opened the door when Walt and Eddy arrived at her villa. Jo perched on the edge of the couch in the living room. She avoided looking at Walt and Eddy.

"All right guys, let's figure this out." Samantha placed the two lists on the dining room table. Jo stood up and joined them at the table. Walt tried to catch her eyes, but Jo busied herself with the lists.

"First, I think Walt has something he'd like to tell us." Eddy leaned his hands against the edge of the table. "Walt?"

Walt sighed and rubbed his hands together. He began to pace beside the table. "I was not completely honest at first. I did not intend to lie, I just didn't think the investigation would be helped by my admission. Now I see that was a mistake." He looked over at Jo again. "I'm sorry if I gave any of you cause to doubt my integrity."

"What?" Samantha frowned. "What are you talking about, Walt?" She glanced around at the rest of her friends. "Why does it seem like I'm the only one who doesn't know?"

"Because you are." Walt cleared his throat. "But not for long. When I worked for Magnus I told you I hesitated to take the job. I knew he was a rough character, that he intimidated people, and I didn't know if I wanted to be part of that. While I worked for him I noticed that some of the employees would lie in order to avoid his wrath. He was vicious when it came to work ethic, more so than anyone I'd ever seen. I let a lot of the discrepancies go, as they did no real harm to the company. However, I came across a flaw in his old financial program that shaved ten percent off several customers' repayments. There was no valid reason for the discount. I could have just let it go, but instead, I brought it to Magnus' attention. He was furious, and determined that someone in his company had gone against his hardline attitude of no discounts, or perhaps was pocketing the difference themselves."

"Did he ever figure out who it was?" Samantha leaned forward across the table. She skimmed the list of names in front of her.

"Unfortunately, I don't think so. He was so irate that he began interrogating his employees. I don't mean just questioning them, I mean interrogating them. When I overheard some of the threats he made, I confronted him and told him I would go to the police if he continued. Of course, I was fired after that." He shrugged. "If I had kept my mouth shut my life would have been easier. But I couldn't ignore what the numbers showed me. I tried to check in on how the employees were after they were fired, but none would speak to me. In fact I was blackballed for quite some time in Magnus' circle. I lost a lot of clients and potential income because of it."

"That's not the story I was told." Jo narrowed her eyes.

"What was the story?" Walt looked over at her

and finally their eyes connected.

"I was told that you found something illegal in Magnus' finances, and you were either intimidated or bribed into keeping your mouth shut."

Walt held her gaze. "Jo, we may not have known each other for long, but I do hope that you know me well enough to see how ridiculous that statement is."

Jo's expression tensed. Everyone looked in her direction. She took a deep breath and then nodded.

"Of course I do, Walt. I'm sorry for ever considering it."

"No need to apologize. If I had explained from the get-go there would not have been any confusion. You'll have to excuse my desire to hide the experience. It's just that it wasn't one of my proudest moments. I'm sure that there was something more I could have done."

"It sounds like you did everything right, Walt.

It's a good thing you stood up for those employees." Samantha patted his shoulder.

"Whoever was stealing from him, might still have some animosity towards Magnus. He might still be an enemy." Jo tapped the table lightly with one finger. "If we can figure out who was stealing then we might just have our murderer."

"Good point, Jo. But first let's talk about these lists," Samantha said. "This one is the list of names I was able to gather for all of the employees that I could find. It includes a few employees who I don't think work there anymore. This one is a list of numbers that I think might coincide with the names."

"They do." Eddy nodded and tapped the sheet of paper. "Chris confirmed it when I was on the phone with him. However, the number that was written down on the paper, doesn't belong to any of the employees on file."

"Oh." Samantha sighed. "I guess that's a dead end then."

"It looks like it is. Chris is going to try to send me the information from keycard swipes around the time of the murder. That should help us narrow down which employees entered the building."

"If they used a keycard." Walt frowned.

"You have to use one to get into the building." Samantha looked across the table at him.

"Maybe, but I've worked at plenty of places where one employee will swipe and then hold the door for an entire group. So, it's possible that more than one person could enter after one keycard swipe."

"That's true." Eddy sat down at the table. "But it looks like an inside job, there was no sign of a break-in and more importantly they also have video surveillance of the police's new suspect."

"Who?" Samantha's eyes widened.

"Jimmy Barker. He was seen on camera entering the building twice last night, once was around the time of the murder. Unfortunately, he also has a very solid alibi for the time of the murder with plenty of witnesses to back him up." Eddy sighed. "He was having dinner with his baseball team."

"How can one person be in two places at once?" Walt shook his head. "That's not possible."

"Sometimes it is." Jo smirked.

"How?" Samantha looked over at her.

"It's easy to look like someone else for the cameras. It's a great way to frame someone or direct attention away from you. A good hat and coat will hide your face and frame easily. If you're lucky you will be able to get the same clothes that the person you are attempting to imitate wears."

"Wait, did you say baseball team?" Samantha picked up the list of employees.

"Yes." Eddy nodded.

"There's a baseball team which some of the employees have formed. Several employees are on it and from what I can tell even a few past employees," Samantha said as she picked up the employee list. "This list includes the baseball players as well as other employees I have managed to find."

Eddy grimaced. "And they are the ones providing Jimmy's alibi. Jimmy claims that his access card was stolen."

"Any one of them could have worn the baseball cap." Walt struck the table with frustration. The sudden sharp sound made everyone at the table jump. "I'm sorry." Walt gulped. "I'm just frustrated."

"It's fine, Walt." Eddy clapped him on the shoulder. "It's okay to be frustrated. It's just that none of us are used to that frustration coming from you."

"I know, I make it my business to try to remain calm at all costs, but this situation is trying my patience."

"It's understandable." Samantha smiled at him.

"No, it's not." Jo crossed her arms. "This is not

the time for any of us to fall apart, especially you, Walt. There's a good chance the police will be back to question you, and if you lose control of your emotions under questioning you will implicate yourself."

"I think Walt's entitled to some emotions." Samantha frowned.

"No, Jo is right." Walt smiled at Samantha. "This is not the time to lose control. I need to remain focused on what is happening here. So, what are we going to do with this list?"

"Well, until we hear from Chris, I think the best chance we have is dividing the list into sections. We can start making calls, arranging interviews." Samantha shrugged. "It's a lot to get through, but it's the only move we have."

"I'm sure that Chris will come through." Eddy checked his cell phone. "Nothing yet."

"We can start making calls until he does," Samantha said.

Jo looked over at Samantha. "I can help you

with that."

"I guess we have our work cut out for us this afternoon." Samantha picked up the list.

"Walt has a list of Jimmy's bank transactions," Eddy explained. "He's going to see if there's anything obviously suspicious about them."

"I'll look into Jimmy as much as possible, too," Samantha said.

"I can also help with the phone calls. Just give me a portion of the list." Walt reached for it, but Eddy interceded before he could.

"Not a good idea. We don't want any calls from you to anyone associated with the company. We don't want to risk anyone recognizing your voice either, Walt. It's important that you keep yourself out of this as much as possible and work behind the scenes." Eddy frowned when he saw his friend's disappointed expression. "Don't worry, Walt, you play your part and look at Jimmy's account records. Let us help you with this part."

"I feel like all I'm doing is letting people help. Not that I'm not grateful, but I hate to cause so much inconvenience."

Samantha stood up and walked over to him. "You're not causing anything, Walt. We're your friends, we want to help." She gave him a light hug.

"Can I at least look at the employee list and the numbers," Walt said. "Maybe there's something we're missing. I won't call anyone."

"Here you go," Samantha said as she handed him a copy of the lists. "If it's something to do with numbers you'll work it out."

"I just wish there was more I could do," Walt said.

"You're doing a lot," Eddy said.

"Keep thinking about anything that you might remember, anything that might help the case," Samantha suggested.

"The clients." Walt's eyes widened. "We should get a list of the clients, too. It's a long shot, but maybe one of the clients wanted to erase their debt."

"That's a lot of trouble to go to just to get out of repaying a loan," Jo remarked. "But I've seen people kill for less."

"I'm going to head down to the station and find out if Chris got any more information yet." Eddy walked towards the door.

"Wouldn't he call you?" Samantha caught up to him and walked with him to the door.

"Sure he would. But there's nothing wrong with applying a little pressure." He winked at Samantha as he stepped out the door. Samantha rolled her eyes and turned back to find that Walt had walked up right behind her.

"I should go, too. I'm not going to be much help here." Walt shrugged.

"Try not to worry too much, Walt, this is all going to get straightened out."

112

"If you say so." Walt nodded. As he left Samantha's villa and walked back towards his, his heart grew heavy. For the thousandth time in his life, he thought about how different things would be if he'd just turned down the job. It was the main reason that he did his best not to always choose money first. Airing his dirty laundry in front of people he cared about was difficult. He hoped their opinions of him hadn't changed. He raised his shoulders up close to his ears as a burst of cool air rushed past him. The question that cycled through his mind was a simple one, who had enough motive and enough anger to kill Magnus?

When Walt arrived at his villa he sat down and looked at the list of numbers. Like Samantha had said there wasn't a number 6886. Walt looked through the numbers slowly. He tapped the page when he reached the number 9889. Was it possible the number on the note had been read upside down? He sent a text to Eddy asking if he could find out who the employee number 9889 was assigned to.

He then looked at the list of employees. Most of the names he didn't recognize, but there were a few he did. He saw the names Chad Hillwick and Len Lazario. Maybe they had returned to work for Magnus' company. If they hadn't then they probably didn't hold any hard feelings towards the company if they were prepared to play with the other employees on the baseball team. Because Walt recognized their names he decided to send a text to Eddy to look into them. Maybe they could provide some information about Jimmy.

While he waited to hear from Eddy or Samantha he decided to do an investigation on Jimmy's life, especially his finances. Yes, he had an alibi, but it might not be as solid as the police thought it was. He launched a few different programs and did a search. The first thing he noticed was just how wealthy Jimmy was. Despite Magnus' reputation for not paying well, Jimmy appeared to have a lot of assets. He looked over the account details that Eddy had given him. He was surprised at how large his paychecks were. Then again he had been with the company for many years. However, his paychecks weren't the only deposits going into his account. There were several smaller deposits throughout the month. Walt followed the trail from the deposit to its source and found that these smaller deposits were coming from a company.

"Hiller Maximum." He looked puzzled. "Why would a company be paying Jimmy for anything?" Walt jotted down the name of the company. Then he began searching for information on the company itself. It was a small business, just the type that Magnus would have snapped up in the past. Maybe the payments were to prevent that? Walt picked up his phone and dialed Samantha's number.

"Hi Walt."

"Hi Samantha. Were you able to find a list of the clients yet?"

"Yes, it's a partial list, but I think we have most of them. One of my contacts who is good with accessing computer systems managed to get it for me. He's still working on getting the rest of the names. Apparently the security at the company is pretty intense."

"Yes, rumor was that Magnus got pretty paranoid after that little discovery that I made. I'm betting he has the best encryption software he can get and maybe a few additional backups to it. On the list that he's given you so far, is there a company by the name of Hiller Maximum?"

"Hiller Maximum?" She paused a moment. "No, I don't see that on here. I do however see a Hiller Brothers."

"Odd. Two companies with similar names? Maybe the owners are relatives?"

"Maybe. I'll see what I can find, Walt."

"Thank you, Samantha." He hung up the phone and looked back at the computer screen. So far he hadn't found anything to prove that Jimmy

116

was involved. But he suspected he was getting closer. By the evening he gave up on the search. He was exhausted and his eyes burned from staring at the computer screen. The only thing he'd dug up was the fact that Jimmy had multiple girlfriends, multiple residences, and a very strong view on politics. If there was anything more than that it would have to wait until the next morning. Just as he was going to get into bed his cell phone rang. He picked it up when he saw that it was Eddy.

"Did you get an update from Chris?"

"Yes eventually, after I got the cold shoulder. He was with some higher ups when I visited, and not too pleased to see me."

"Is everything okay?"

"Yes, it is. He met with me afterwards and told me that they're pulling out all of the stops to get the case solved, including getting him directly involved. It may be a little harder to get information from him as he will be more closely monitored."

"Well, that makes things harder." Walt sighed.

"It does. He also told me that the employee number 9889 belongs to a Kent Waltet."

"Interesting, it's a long shot but it's worth looking into. What about Chad Hillwick and Len Lazario?"

"I almost forgot. He also mentioned that they were at the baseball game and then the dinner with Jimmy around the time of the murder. No one could verify with complete certainty whether any of the players were at the dinner the whole time, but they were at least there for most of the time so it's still quite a solid alibi."

"That's a dead end then."

"Looks like it. Samantha called me a little while ago and said she only managed to reach a few employees, and none agreed to talk to her."

"That makes it even harder." Walt closed his eyes.

"I know it seems like we're hitting nothing but dead ends. If only there was a way we could get together with a group of employees. Maybe we could hit one of their baseball games."

Walt's eyes widened. "Wait a minute, I know where we could go. There's a restaurant near the company that most of the employees would go to for lunch. I don't know if they still do, but it might be worth a shot."

"Great idea, Walt. We can go there tomorrow for lunch and try to get some information."

"You want me to go with you? Aren't you afraid someone will recognize me?"

"At this point I'm more interested in you recognizing people. Since Magnus never discovered who was stealing from him, that we know of, the employees that have been there the longest might be a good group of suspects. If you can point out people you are familiar with I can focus on them for questioning."

"You are a genius you know that, Eddy?"

"Sure, this from the man who casually recreates a computer program in an afternoon. This is all going to be over soon."

"I hope so. I'm not sure if I'm going to be able to sleep until it is."

"Warm milk and a shot of vodka, works every time. Trust me."

"I'm not much of a drinker."

"Do you want to sleep or not?"

"Yes, I do." Walt closed his eyes. "Thanks Eddy." He hung up the phone and sat down on the edge of his bed. If he had vodka, he might have tried Eddy's idea. But he didn't. Instead he stretched out on his bed and began counting as high as he could. It was a trick he used as a child to get himself to fall asleep. He counted pretty high.

Chapter Nine

Eddy stared out through the windshield. Walt was silent beside him. The morning was gray. Drips of rain struck the windshield. No good news came that morning. It was just another day closer to the police deciding whether to arrest Walt or not. Eddy pulled into the parking lot of the restaurant that Walt had pointed out.

"I can't believe it's still here. It's funny, I only worked briefly for Magnus, but some things I remember vividly."

"Is the food good?" Eddy locked the car doors as they walked up to the restaurant.

"As I recall it was decent, and you know how I am about restaurant food."

"Yes, it surprises me that you would go out to lunch every day."

"I only worked there part-time, but trust me, if you had felt the tension in that building you too would have gotten out every chance you had." Walt pulled out a tissue from his pocket and covered his hand with it before he opened the door. Eddy walked through. A young girl in a yellow uniform walked up to them.

"Table for two?"

Eddy pointed to the small bar near the front of the restaurant. "Actually, could we sit there?"

"Sure, if you like. Pick your spot and you can order from the bartender."

"Thanks." Eddy glanced over at Walt. "It'll give us the best view of the entire restaurant."

"Good idea." Walt followed him over to the bar. There were quite a few people in the restaurant. The noise level was still tolerable.

"Did you make friends with anyone from the company?" Eddy looked around the restaurant again.

"Not exactly. I was more the type to keep to myself."

"Understood." Eddy nodded. "Well, if any of the workers still blow off steam here maybe we'll get lucky."

"I hope so." Walt wiped his seat and the counter in front of him with a wipe before he sat down. Eddy was so used to Walt's behavior that he barely noticed.

"Can I get you something?" The bartender paused in front of them.

"Room temperature water please."

The bartender raised an eyebrow. "All right. You, Sir?" He looked at Eddy.

"I'll take a soda if you have one."

"Sure, no problem."

"Any familiar faces?" Eddy glanced around at the people that were gathered at the tables for lunch.

"It's been years, Eddy. I'm sure that the people I worked with then, don't work there anymore."

"Magnus was still there." Eddy took off his hat and set it on the bar.

"Yes, but Magnus rarely kept an employee beyond a few years. The place had a high turnover rate."

"See, you know more about the company than you realize."

"Maybe I do." Walt sighed and took his glass of water. "I just think that we're at a dead end here."

"Don't think that way. We're going to come up with something, trust me."

Just as Eddy took a sip of his soda the door to the restaurant swung open. The moment the man walked in, a cheer went up from a crowded table. The man paused near the door. His cheeks turned pink. He lowered his eyes. Eddy watched him as he walked across the restaurant towards the table. A few of the people at the table stood up to greet him.

"Oh, wait a minute, I think I know her." Walt

narrowed his eyes at the woman who gave the man a hug. "She looks like the receptionist that worked with Magnus. In fact, I would bet my life on it. She was the one employee that he actually liked, it would make sense that she would still be at the company."

"Which makes me wonder who the man is that she is hugging."

"I don't know, he's too young for me to remember him. He looks like he's in his twenties."

"Hm." Eddy stood up from the chair. "Only one way to find out."

"Eddy, what are you doing?"

"I'm going to find out who that man is and why they are cheering for him."

Walt took a sip of his water. A deep breath followed a hard swallow. Eddy paused beside the table.

"Congratulations." He smiled at the man who had just sat down.

"I'm sorry?" The man looked over at him.

"Oh, I just thought with all of the cheering congratulations were in order."

"Not exactly." The receptionist smiled at him. "We're just glad he's okay."

"Yeah." The man rubbed his hand back through his hair. "It's been a rough couple of days."

"Don't be modest." The receptionist shot him a reproachful look, then turned back to Eddy. "Our company was broken into, and Kent here survived. He was knocked out by the intruder, but he managed to make it out of there alive. So we're celebrating that." Eddy's eyes widened at the mention of the man's name. The number 9889 was assigned to a Kent.

"Oh, I'm so sorry to intrude. Sounds like you are a brave young man, Kent." He smiled at Kent.

"Not exactly." Kent sighed. "All I did was get knocked out."

"Must have hurt." Eddy scrutinized his

126

features.

"It did." Kent's voice grew quiet. "But I feel better already. I'm back at work tonight."

"Well, you have a reason to celebrate. Enjoy." Eddy turned and walked away from the table. As soon as he was a few feet away the chatter at the table began again. Eddy joined Walt at the bar again.

"Looks like that's our only witness," Eddy said.

"The employee that was working?" Walt asked.

"Yes. He claims he was knocked out."

"You don't think he was?"

"I think when someone is knocked out cold, they have a mark of some kind on them. I didn't see a knot, or a black eye, or anything to indicate that he was assaulted."

"Maybe it was a blow to the back of the head? It's hard to see beyond the hair," Walt said.

"I doubt it. He rubbed his head and didn't even flinch. If you're hit hard enough to get knocked out, the pain lingers for a couple of days at least."

"I guess that you're right about that. I wonder if the police report noted anything about injuries."

"I can check on that," Eddy said. "There's another thing."

"What?" Walt asked eagerly.

"His name is Kent. He is probably the same Kent that has the employee number 9889."

"Oh." Walt's eyes widened.

"That might explain why Magnus wrote it down," Eddy said. "Because he was there when Magnus was murdered."

"Or maybe because he was the murderer."

"I'll just be a minute," Eddy said as he stood up and walked towards the restroom. Walt had his eyes on the people at the table. When Eddy walked away, Walt stood up and walked towards the table. He took a seat a few feet away so that he could hear their conversation.

"Look guys, I really appreciate this, but I don't deserve it. All I did was get knocked out," Kent said.

"Are you kidding?" The man sitting beside him shook his head. "I'd be scared to even walk back in that building if it happened to me. Heck, I'm scared to walk back in after what happened to Magnus. If a man like that could be killed, then anyone is game."

"It's not like he didn't have it coming." Another woman at the table tilted her head back. "He made more enemies than friends."

"Watch it, Cheryl, that's no way to talk about Mr. Magnus." The receptionist huffed.

"Please, Madeline, we all know that you were his favorite. I'm not saying anything bad about the man, I'm just being realistic. Whoever did this clearly wanted Magnus dead. Why else would he have left Kent alive?"

"Ouch." Kent frowned. "I'd rather not think about what else could have happened."

"I'm sorry, you're right," Cheryl apologized. "I just can't help but wonder who might have been after him. Do you think the murderer might come back?"

"Cheryl, enough." Madeline smacked her hand on the table. "You're getting everyone all worked up. There's no reason for that."

"I'm not trying to cause any trouble, but I think I have the right to be concerned about whether we will be safe at work," Cheryl said. "Obviously security isn't tight enough."

"She's right," Kent agreed. "No one should have been able to just walk in there."

"Unless they belonged there." Madeline clucked her tongue.

"What are you saying?" Kent looked over at her. "You think it was an inside job?"

"I don't just think it. I know it." Madeline swept her gaze around the table. "It could have even been one of you sitting right here."

The table fell into silence at the comment. Cheryl scrunched up her nose. "Yes, it could have been you. I've always wondered about the two of you. Are the rumors true?"

"Rumors?" Madeline scowled at her. "What rumors?"

A few guilty looks were exchanged around the table before Cheryl spoke up again. "About you and Magnus. Were you together?"

"Magnus was married."

"And?" Cheryl laughed. "His wife lives in another state."

"You seem to know an awful lot about a man you didn't even consider your friend, Cheryl." Madeline pushed her chair back from the table. "I am not going to sit here and be ridiculed by you. A man is dead, and all you can think about is flapping your gums. Ridiculous." She shook her head. Cheryl held up her hands.

"I was just asking a question."

"You'd better watch yourself." Kent pointed a finger at her. "With Jimmy as acting CEO none of our jobs are safe. Be careful who you make angry."

"I am already looking for another job. I don't want to work for Jimmy any more than I wanted to work for Magnus. You know that Jimmy's been dying to get in this position for a while now. I can only imagine what kind of power trip he'll be on now that he's in it." Cheryl pursed her lips and then released a heavy sigh. "It's not like the pay is great anyway."

"True." Kent raised a glass. "I can toast to that."

"We all can." The man beside him raised his glass as well. Soon the entire group at the table held their glasses in the air. The ensuing clinks made Walt cringe and draw back. Certain sounds always set off his nerves. Walt stood and walked back over to meet Eddy back at the bar.

"Where did you go?"

"To eavesdrop."

132

"Hear anything good?"

"Magnus' receptionist is still the same woman, and there are rumors that she might have had an affair with him. I think we should talk to her."

Eddy smiled. "Then we will. What's her name?"

"Madeline." Walt frowned. "I'm not sure that she'll talk to us though."

"Oh, don't worry, she'll talk." He stood up from the bar and watched as the woman left the table. She seemed a little annoyed as she headed for the door. Eddy casually fell into step behind her. He didn't quicken his pace until she was outside the restaurant. Walt trailed right after him. Just as Madeline paused beside a late model silver car Eddy walked up to her.

"Excuse me, Madeline?"

She turned to face him. "Yes?" She looked into his eyes with a hint of confusion.

"I'm sorry, I don't mean to startle you. My

friend Walt here, told me your name." He smiled. Walt stood a few steps away from her and offered a nervous smile.

"Walt?" She narrowed her eyes as she looked at him. All of a sudden her expression shifted. "Walt Right?"

Walt swallowed hard. "Yes, that's me. I mean, it's me."

"It's been years! How are you?"

"Uh, not the best at the moment actually." He looked down at his shoes.

"Right, I heard that the police are looking into you." She laughed. "When they questioned me about you I nearly choked on my coffee. As if Walt Right would ever hurt anyone."

Eddy looked between the two with a raised eyebrow.

"Thank you for that, Madeline. I wasn't sure if you would remember me."

"I remember." Her smile spread wider. "You

were the most honest man I'd ever met. I'd never seen anyone stand up to Magnus like that before."

"That didn't bother you?" Eddy broke the spell between the two as they gazed at each other. "Weren't you and Magnus close?"

"Don't believe the rumor mill, Sir. I've always believed that work and personal life should be kept separate. Magnus had some preferences that gave off a certain image of our relationship, but it was strictly professional."

"I'm sorry for your loss." Walt frowned. "You two worked together for so long."

"Oh trust me, it was no great loss." Madeline pursed her lips. "I know I'm not supposed to say that, but to be honest I feel free for the first time in decades."

"Madeline." Walt stepped closer to her. "Did he do something to hurt you?"

"It's water under the bridge. The important thing is just to move on from here."

"Walt isn't going to be able to do that if he's in

handcuffs." Eddy tightened his hands at his sides. "If you know something that can help us, you should tell us."

"What could I know?" Madeline's eyes widened. "Are you a police officer?"

"He's a good friend of mine." Walt's tone softened. "He's just trying to help me out of this mess."

"I see." Madeline nodded a little. "That's a good thing. You don't deserve any of this, Walt."

"Then maybe you could tell us what you know about Jimmy Barker?" Eddy moved to the other side of her to prevent her access to her car.

"Jimmy?" Madeline rolled her eyes. "He's all bluster. He loves to push people around because Magnus has always pushed him around."

"Wouldn't he have wanted Magnus out of the way?" Eddy pressed. Walt watched him closely.

"Everyone wanted Magnus out of the way. But Jimmy's not a killer." Madeline shrugged.

"Are you sure about that?" Eddy narrowed his eyes.

"Are you trying to say that I might be lying?" She glared right back.

"Eddy, please." Walt stepped between them. Eddy grimaced, but Walt ignored him. He looked into Madeline's eyes. "I don't think that you're lying, Madeline. I'm sorry we've bothered you. I have one question for you. Is that okay?"

"Sure." She relaxed as she met his gaze.

"Hiller Brothers and Hiller Maximum, do you know anything about those two companies?" Walt asked.

She grappled for her door handle. "Walt, I always liked you. Please, listen to me when I tell you. Do not get involved with the Hillers. They are very powerful people. That is all I will say about it."

"Madeline, can't you tell me anything more?" Walt asked.

"Excuse me, I'd like to leave now." She

elbowed Eddy out of her way and opened the door to her car. "Good luck, Walt." She glanced back once at him. "I mean it."

"Thank you, Madeline."

"Walt." Eddy grimaced. Walt closed the door for her and then stepped away from the car. As she pulled away Eddy looked over at him. "Our best lead just drove away."

Walt pursed his lips then glanced over at Eddy. "She's still a lady, Eddy, and we're not going to pressure her. If she has more to say, there are other ways we can find out."

"Obviously those two companies are a red flag. It's time we get together with Samantha and Jo to discuss this."

He pulled out his cell phone and dialed Samantha's number. When she answered he tried to hide the frustration in his voice.

"Can you and Jo meet us for lunch?"

"Sure. When and where?"

"Now, and I'll text you the address."

"We'll be there as soon as we can."

Eddy hung up the phone and texted her the address of the restaurant. Then he raised his eyes back to Walt.

"Listen Walt, I want your name cleared. But if we're going to make that happen, you're going to have to be willing to take a few chances."

"I am." Walt wiped the hand that touched the car door handle with a wipe. "But not with Madeline."

"Is there something I should know?" Eddy raised his eyebrows.

"Nothing ever happened."

"Remember, a woman can be just as dangerous as a man, Walt, and it seems that she has motive, by her own admission she didn't like the man."

"I hear you, Eddy. Trust me, I've never been one to be dazzled by a pretty face."

"It is a pretty one though isn't it?" Eddy winked at him. Walt rolled his eyes.

"I can't say that I noticed."

"Yeah right." He shook his head. "Let's go back in and wait for the girls."

"Women, Eddy, women."

"Yeah, yeah." Eddy grinned.

Chapter Ten

As Eddy and Walt settled at a table to wait for Samantha and Jo Walt looked towards the bartender. He waved and the bartender walked over.

"Sorry, I'm going off shift. Arlene will take care of you at the bar." He pointed to a woman who tugged an apron over her head. "Or you can order from Becs," he said as he pointed to the waitress.

"Okay that's fine, thank you." Walt nodded. "I just wanted to know if you're very familiar with that crew that just left."

"Oh sure. They come in here for lunch a lot."

"Just lunch?" Eddy leaned forward. "Do they ever come in for anything else?"

"Not really, not as a group. Sometimes a few of them will come in alone for dinner or a drink." He shrugged.

"Thanks." Eddy handed him a few dollars as a tip. The bartender walked away.

Eddy rubbed his hand along his chin. "What is it?" Walt looked over at him.

"I just can't get over how uninjured Kent appeared. He didn't even seem that shaken up by the experience."

"Maybe he was still in shock," Walt said.

"Maybe, but I'm going to put in a call to Chris. I want to see if he can get a copy of the medical records from that night. If Kent was injured he likely would have gone to the hospital, or maybe he got checked out by paramedics."

"Good idea."

Eddy dialed Chris' number. Within moments he answered the phone.

"Eddy, it's good to hear from you."

"Do you really mean that?" Eddy waved to Samantha and Jo as they stepped into the restaurant.

"Of course I do. What are you looking for?"

"Do you have any medical records for the night shift employee that was knocked out? Kent?"

"No, I don't have any. As far as I know there weren't any medical records."

"Why is that? A man gets knocked out but no hospital visit?"

"He refused medical care."

"What about paramedics? Photographs of the injury?"

"None that I can find."

"Chris, did someone drop the ball?"

"I don't really know. But I can tell you that he insisted he woke up only after his boss was dead. I'm sure if the detective suspected him they would have investigated the issue further."

"Just like they documented the injuries?"

"Good point." Chris yawned. "I'm sorry, it's been a long night. I'll see what I can do about finding out why nothing more was done to confirm his story. Anything else I can help you with right now?"

"No thanks, that's all I needed. I appreciate your help."

"Oh, you're going to owe me. I'm still waiting to find out everything that happened with the investigation of that double murder you worked in ninety-two."

"In time, in time." Eddy chuckled. Samantha and Jo joined them at the table. Walt signaled for the waitress to come over. The woman smiled at them as she approached.

"Hi, what can I get for you?"

Eddy tucked his phone into his pocket. "I'll take a soda, and some cheese fries."

"Eddy." Samantha clucked her tongue. "You remember what Owen said the last time you had a check-up." Owen was the young nurse at Sage Gardens who had become Eddy's friend.

Eddy looked around the restaurant. "I'm

sorry, I didn't see him here, when did he come in?"

"So, no cheese fries?" The bartender hovered her pen over the notepad in her hand. "Does anyone want cheese fries?"

"I do." Eddy cleared his throat. "Add a little bacon if you can, too."

Samantha pursed her lips.

"Can I get a beer please?" Jo set her purse on the floor beneath the table. She hooked her foot through the strap.

"Sure. Any cheese fries?"

"No, I'll just eat his." Jo winked at Eddy.

"That's what you think." Eddy glowered at her.

"Let's focus here, please," Walt said. After they finished placing their order the four leaned closer. Eddy updated Samantha and Jo on what they had overheard, and their suspicion of Kent. When he tried to mention Madeline as a suspect,

Walt interrupted.

"She's worked with him for decades. If she wanted him dead, I'm sure there would be much easier ways for her to accomplish that. Why would she do something so messy?"

"Maybe because she wanted it to look like the murderer was caught doing something he shouldn't be?" Jo shrugged. "It's possible."

"Yes, it is possible." Samantha nodded. "She would have wanted it to seem as if someone else entirely did it, so that not even an ounce of suspicion would be cast on her."

"Maybe, but that doesn't mean that she did it." Walt folded his hands on the table.

"And it doesn't mean that she didn't." Samantha twirled a napkin between her fingers. "We need to think about the motive here. Clearly Jimmy had motive, he would benefit from Magnus' death."

"And Madeline would finally be out from under his thumb." Eddy looked over at Walt.

146

"And Kent could have easily lied about being knocked out." Walt insisted. "What did you find out from Chris?"

"Just that there are no records of Kent actually being injured. No pictures, no medical evaluation, nothing but his own word," Eddy said.

"That's odd." Samantha tapped a finger against the table. "If I was injured by someone at work, I'd want that medical evaluation. I'd want to prove that it happened while I was on duty. That way I might be able to get worker's compensation, or even better file a lawsuit against a very wealthy company."

"Maybe he's just an honest guy." Jo shrugged. "I know that's a stretch because of how sue happy everyone is these days, but it might be possible, right?"

"Maybe." Eddy looked up at the ceiling for a moment. "Well, one thing we do know is that Jimmy's keycard was missing, or so he claims. If he really didn't hide it or get rid of it in an attempt to make himself look like a victim, then maybe someone else took it. They might have even been an employee and took Jimmy's card so they didn't have to use their own card and draw attention to themselves or maybe they even took it to implicate Jimmy in the murder. Whoever has it, is likely to be our killer."

"So, you want me to get into Kent's house?" Jo snatched one of Eddy's cheese fries before the dish even settled on the table.

"Hey." Eddy sighed.

"It's one of the perks." She stole another one. Once the waitress was gone Eddy nodded at her.

"Yes, I think a look around Kent's house would be a good idea. He's the easiest suspect to access and a good place to start. Maybe we'll find something that implicates him, or we'll find something to clear him. Whichever it is, it will help the investigation."

"I'm sure I can handle breaking into his place." Jo popped another fry into her mouth.

"Seriously, the two of you are eating like teenagers. We don't have the luxury of ignoring our digestive systems." Samantha shook her head.

"You may know a lot of things about me, Samantha, but my digestive system is something we will never discuss." Eddy grinned.

Samantha sighed. "I'll look up Kent's house so we can get an idea of how we can approach this." She tapped the screen of her phone.

"Do you think there's a way we can get into Madeline's?" Eddy shot a look over at Walt.

"I don't think that's wise. She might be living alone, she was when I worked at the company. If we were to be caught breaking in, there would be a lot of wrong ideas," Walt said. "Let's take this one suspect at a time."

"Hey pal, it's your life on the line. These detectives are chomping at the bit to get someone in custody and put Magnus to rest. We may not have the luxury of taking our time." Eddy furrowed a brow. "She doesn't have to know that you were involved."

"Eddy, let's focus on Kent." Walt picked up his glass. "That's that."

Eddy sat back in his chair. He moved his mouth slightly as if he might speak again, but in the end silenced himself with a cheese fry.

"Here it is." Samantha held up her phone for everyone at the table to see the picture on it. "It's a townhouse, so there will be neighbors and limited entrances. But there is a balcony on the back of the house." She flipped to another picture that displayed the back of the house.

"Oh look." Jo smirked and pointed out an overflowing ashtray in the corner of the balcony. "A smoker. This might be easier than I expected. Always ducking out for a smoke break often means forgetting to lock the door behind you."

"All right, then I guess we strike tonight?" Eddy looked around the table at each of them.

"Meanwhile, I think we should dig deeper into this connection with Hiller Brothers and Hiller

Maximum. I really believe there could be something there," Walt said. "Can you see if you can get a printout of the financial transactions for both companies from Chris for me please, Eddy?"

"All right, I'll try." Eddy nodded at Walt. "Let's all call it a day. Samantha, if you can dig any deeper into Kent's social media profiles that would be great. Since he works the night shift, and he said he will be back to work tonight, we shouldn't have to worry about him walking in on the break-in. Jo, do you need any supplies?"

"No, I have it covered, but thanks for asking."

"Well, since I'm supplying you my cheese fries, I thought perhaps I'd make a habit of it."

"Ha ha." Jo took the last fry out of the dish.

"Cruel." Eddy shook his head. As the four left the restaurant Eddy hung back and caught Samantha by the arm. "A moment?"

"Sure." She met his eyes with a small smile. "If it's about what I said about Owen, I'm sorry. That wasn't my business to share with the group."

"I'm not worried about that. Owen thinks we're all dying, he's young enough not to realize that a little bit of creak in the bones is just a sign of a good life. I need to ask you to do something, but I'd prefer that you keep it between us. I've noticed that Walt is a little sensitive about the topic and I don't want to do anything to upset him more than he already is."

"Okay, what is it?" She inquired.

"The receptionist, Madeline, has worked with Magnus for a very long time. I'm sure she knows just about everyone he did, and everything about him. If you could dig into her social media presence, maybe even her personal files, whatever you can access, that might be able to tell us something."

"What's the back story? Did she and Walt have a thing?"

"I'm guessing it was more of a missed romance."

"Ah. Those are tough, especially when you see

the person again."

"That's true, but this person that he's seeing again might just be a murderer. So let's find out what we can about her. If we don't find anything on Kent tonight, then we're going to need to look into her house next. Breaking into Jimmy's would be a last resort as the police already have an eye on him."

"Okay, no problem. I'll let you know what I find out."

"And like I said, try not to mention it to Walt."

"I won't." Samantha's gaze lingered on his. "I think it's good that you're so worried about his feelings."

"I think it's frustrating that the investigation has to be slowed because of it."

"Walt is a very delicate man." Samantha looked out through the door of the restaurant at Walt opening the door to her car for Jo.

"Most of us are." Eddy patted her shoulder, then held the restaurant door open for her. "Let's get out there before they get suspicious."

As he walked up to Jo he caught the door before Walt could shut it. "So tonight, we'll meet at nine? Walt, it's best if you stay home. If this goes south I don't want you anywhere near it."

"Oh, but it's just fine if I'm caught red-handed?" Jo laughed. "I'm just kidding. Eddy's right, Walt. It's best for you to be as predictable as possible."

"Well, that shouldn't be too hard." Walt laughed.

Eddy walked over to the car with him. Just when they were about to get into the car, Walt looked across the top of it at him.

"It's strange, Eddy."

"What is?"

"For years, I worked with hundreds of people. I have met so many people in my lifetime, but it wasn't until I moved to Sage Gardens and met the three of you that I had any true friends."

"I don't think that's strange at all, Walt. I find myself feeling the same way."

"Then I hope that you will trust me when I tell you, Madeline wasn't involved in any of this. I'd rather she not think that I suspect her."

"Don't worry, Buddy, I'm not going to do anything to ruin your second chance."

"It's not like that, Eddy."

"If you say so."

Chapter Eleven

Eddy dropped Walt off at his villa. Walt turned back to thank him, but Eddy drove away before he could. No matter what his friend said, Walt suspected that he was not too happy with him. Not that he could really blame him. Walt had been evasive, and that was the worst way to be during an investigation. He unlocked the door to his villa, then stepped inside. With his mind still buzzing from the conversation with Madeline he paced through his living room.

Each time he closed his eyes even for just a second he relived moments of time that he had spent working for Magnus. So much of that time involved Madeline. He always had to go through her to get to Magnus, everyone did. A thought floated through his mind. The moment it did, he wished it hadn't. Was it possible that Madeline decided once and for all to rid herself of the overbearing man that pinned his employees beneath his thumb? Maybe she didn't have the heart to do it herself, but she would probably have the means to hire someone else.

Walt settled at the computer and reluctantly opened a few of the tools that he used to investigate the finances of people and businesses. He didn't want Eddy to investigate Madeline, but that meant he needed to investigate her himself.

As Walt began to look for information on Madeline, his mouth grew dry. It was simply not the same to look into someone's life that he knew, as it was to look through a stranger's. Each time he found information about her his stomach flipped. It was not his business what she spent her money on. It was not for him to know that she had recently bought a new house, unless she decided to tell him. He closed his eyes and wiped his fingers across the lids.

"What are you doing, Walt? She didn't have anything to do with this." Instead of looking any further he shut the computer down. All of the suspicion that swirled around him was making him lose his focus. The attention needed to be where it belonged, on Jimmy. He recalled the small payments from Hiller Maximum. There had to be a reason for them. Jimmy wasn't receiving payments from any other company, so it was unlikely that he was engaged in freelance work. Not to mention that there was another company that appeared to belong to the same person or at least the same family. It was quite suspicious from any direction that he looked at it. He picked up his phone and dialed Samantha's number.

"Hi Walt, how are you holding up?"

"I'm doing okay. Any luck so far?"

"No, not really." She sighed. "I can't seem to get any good information."

"Could you maybe take a break and look into something for me?"

"Sure, what is it?" Samantha asked.

"There's a company called Hiller Maximum. Anything you can find on it would be great."

"And the reason you're looking into it?"

"I'll let you know after you tell me what you find. It may be nothing, but I want to be able to cross it off my list," Walt said.

"Okay, no problem. I'll give you a call if I find anything."

"I wish I could be there with you guys tonight."

"I know you do, but this is something that we have to do without you. Don't worry I'll be sure to call you with an update as soon as we leave."

"Good. Thank you so much, Samantha. I don't know what I would do without all of you."

"You're not going to have to find out, Walt. That's why we're all working together, to keep you safe."

"I just wish I could do more myself."

"You'd be surprised how much you really are doing. Just try to be patient with yourself, Walt. When the time comes I am quite certain that you will have the key evidence to break the case."

159

"Sure. Talk to you later, Samantha." He hung up the phone before he could say anything more. Samantha was only trying to help, but he was exhausted by how much help he needed. All he really wanted was to crack the case completely on his own.

Walt pulled off his tie and sat down on the edge of his bed. It was too early for a nap really, but he was exhausted. The intensity of the investigation took more out of him than he expected. As he gazed towards the window he thought about his time with Magnus. He never really took the time to get to know the man, not that Magnus would have allowed it. But he wondered how Madeline endured working for someone like him for so many years. Was it really just about the money? Was there something more between them? He grimaced as he realized that he was beginning to think like Eddy. His fingertips glided across the comforter beneath him to smooth out the wrinkles he created by sitting on it. There was nothing to smooth out the wrinkles in his mind though.

The more Walt thought about it, the more certain he was that the investigation would begin to target him. Jimmy had an alibi, and it appeared as if no one even thought of Kent as a suspect. The more he thought about it, the more frightened he became. He kicked off his shoes, then picked them up and placed them neatly under the bottom of the bed frame. Then he stretched out on the bed. In his mind he counted down the seconds that it should take for him to fall asleep. He knew every little pattern that he had. He had so many years to get to know himself, and so few to get to know anyone else. Yet somehow Madeline sparked an interest in him.

Walt closed his eyes and took a deep breath. He lost count and had to begin again. With the numbers whirring through his mind he began to grow sleepy. Just as he was about to drift off into sleep, his cell phone began to ring. He yawned and forced himself to sit up. He was sure that it had to be Eddy calling with an update on the case.

However, the phone number was unfamiliar to him. He considered ignoring it as he was quite certain that it would be a sales call, but something compelled him to answer.

"This is Walt."

"Hi Walt."

He pressed the phone against his ear. Could it be who he thought it was? "Madeline?"

"Yes, it's me. I'm sorry, I know that I probably shouldn't be calling."

"Why are you?" His tone was more abrupt than he intended. "I'm sorry, I mean it's fine that you call."

"It really isn't. With the murder I know what your friend was trying to ask me today."

"Please don't let him bother you, he's a retired police officer and is more accustomed to interrogation than conversation."

"I noticed that." She laughed. "Thank you for the reassurance. Still, it's unfair of me to put you in this position."

"What position is that?"

She took a long, audible breath. He raised an eyebrow and waited for her response. "The truth is, I wanted to call you for personal reasons."

"Personal reasons? I'm not sure I understand."

"Walt, when we worked together, I know it was a very long time ago, but I really enjoyed it."

"So did I."

"When you stood up to Magnus the way you did, you made a huge impression on me."

"Oh?" Walt smiled a little. "It was one of my braver moments."

"It was more than brave. It was bold, and determined, and so very good of you."

He tightened his grip on the phone. "I still don't understand what this is about."

"It's about the fact that I developed a crush on you back then."

"A crush?" He laughed.

"I'm serious."

His laughter faded. "You can't be."

"But I am. I hoped the entire time on that last day that you would ask me out, or at least ask for my phone number. I was too shy to ask you then and I've always regretted it."

"Madeline, I had no idea."

"I don't know how you didn't see it. I practically fell all over myself to try to make it clear."

"I thought that you were just being kind. I didn't realize." He sighed. "Wow, I wish I had."

"Me too." She cleared her throat. "But now, all this time later, we are thrust back into each others' lives. It makes me wonder if there might be something deeper at work here."

"I think it is pretty amazing that we have been reunited, I just wish it had been under different circumstances."

"Yes, that is unfortunate. I was wondering if you could meet me for dinner."

Walt glanced at his watch. He wasn't supposed to be there when Jo broke in. He could either sit at home alone and obsess over the case, or he could take a chance and have dinner with a woman who remembered him after so long.

"Sure, I can do that. Where?"

"Pacific?"

"What time?"

"About seven?"

He cringed at the approximate time. He needed to know the hour, the minute, even the second if possible.

"Uh huh, seven. Okay, I'll be there."

"Great. We'll talk then."

As soon as Walt hung up the phone he realized what a mistake he'd made. He agreed to go to dinner with a woman who Eddy considered to be one of the main suspects in Magnus' murder.

The main problem he had though was that he had to figure out what to wear. He hadn't been on a date in a very long time. Was it a date? Did he want it to be a date? The amount of things that he couldn't pin down made him feel queasy. It was hard enough to believe that Madeline might want to spend some social time with him. What about what she had to say. Was it something about the case? He gritted his teeth and began to sort through the clothes in his closet. The only way to find out was to go out with her. If he let his nerves prevent him from going then he would never know what she had to say. Once he settled on a suit he combed his hair, brushed, flossed, rinsed his mouth, and spent some time grooming his fingernails. It was a routine he usually saved only for the mornings and evenings, but this was a special occasion. It wasn't often that he got a second chance.

Chapter Twelve

Eddy glanced at his watch and frowned. "Are you sure she said she was on her way?"

"Yes Eddy, please try to calm down, she's only a few minutes late," Samantha said.

"A few minutes can mean everything. What if Kent comes back early?"

"He won't. He has to finish his shift."

"Still."

"Look, there she is now." Samantha pointed to a car as it pulled into the driveway of the empty parking lot.

"About time." Eddy frowned. Jo stepped out of the car and hurried up to them. She always surprised Samantha when she saw her dressed for a break-in. She was dressed in skin-tight black clothes with her long, black hair tied in a tight ponytail. She looked impeccable as always.

"I'm sorry I'm late." She looked at Eddy, who

looked down at his watch, then back up at her. "I needed to pick up a few more things for tonight."

"Are you all set now?" Samantha pulled her phone out of her purse. "I can get anything else you might need."

"No, I should be fine. We can head right in."

"Okay. I went ahead and put a little tracker on Kent's car," Samantha said.

"You did?" Eddy raised an eyebrow. "When did you do that?"

"You don't need to know all of my secrets, Eddy." Samantha smiled. "It should let me know when Kent is headed home. That way there's not so much risk to Jo."

"How thoughtful of you, Samantha." Jo smiled at her. "Well then, I'll get to work." She saluted Eddy and jogged out of the parking lot. Eddy and Samantha followed several feet behind. They made their way to a spot they'd chosen earlier. It was a small bus stop, close enough to Kent's residence to keep an eye on Jo. Not only did the bus stop offer them shelter, it provided them with a reason for being there.

"Do you think she'll find anything?" Samantha watched as Jo disappeared.

"I hope so. We need a break in this case, fast. I know that it's weighing heavily on Walt."

"I think it's more than just the case. The memories of the past are bothering him," Samantha said.

"I imagine they would. Working for Magnus was no treat," Eddy said.

"Neither was never having his chance with Madeline."

Eddy looked over at her. "Do you really think that's what's getting to him?"

"Who knows with Walt? He doesn't exactly let anyone in. The important thing is that he knows we support him. As long as he knows that, he'll be fine," Samantha said.

Eddy pursed his lips and looked in the

direction of Kent's house. "Maybe we should have let him be here tonight."

"I think it's best that he isn't. Until his name is cleared, he's got to stay out of sight. No need to tempt the detective into arresting him."

"You're right." Eddy nodded. He pulled out his phone and checked it for any new messages from Chris. Maybe he would come up with something to break the case. Or maybe he would at least be able to give him some insight as to why Magnus was killed. There wasn't a single voice message or text.

***

Jo rounded the side of the townhouse and headed for the back. Getting to the balcony would be easy enough for her. There was a drainpipe that she climbed easily. When she jumped down onto the balcony, the loud thump of her feet made her cringe. Perhaps she was a bit rusty. Or maybe in her rush to make it on time she'd forgotten to take a few calming breaths and focus. The loud noise reminded her that she was still at risk, even with the tracker on Kent's car, even with her friends only a few steps away. She took a moment to breathe deeply.

After a little fiddling with the handle on the balcony door, Jo found that as she had hoped, the door was unlocked. She stepped inside and closed the door behind her. The interior was messy. Clothes hung over the back of the couch, dirty dishes were strewn across the coffee table. She made her way through the DVD collection, and the assortment of mostly untouched books on a small shelf. Nothing caught her interest. She skipped the kitchen and headed for the bedroom.

When Jo opened the bedroom door she was greeted by a stale odor. Perhaps he didn't change his sheets much, or maybe there was a stray plate of food tucked away somewhere and forgotten for far too long. Either way, it urged her to complete her task quickly. Right away she noticed an overflowing laundry basket. It was the best place to look. She tried to ignore the fact that the crumpled up clothes were at least a week overdue for a wash as she dug through the pile. She ran her fingers through the pockets of each of the shirts and pants. If Kent had Jimmy's card, then he would be the main suspect without question. What a great way to frame someone for the murder, use their keycard. When she reached the bottom of the laundry basket she felt something hard. A smile spread across her lips.

"There it is." She fished out the item with mounting confidence. However, when she pulled it out she found that it was just the cardboard tag still attached to a t-shirt.

"Really? New, clean clothes mixed with dirty clothes, Kent? Yuck." She shook her head and tossed all of the clothes back into the basket. She doubted there was any chance that Kent would notice a difference in the pile, but it was always good to be careful. As she walked away from the laundry basket she noticed that his bedroom closet was half-open. She pulled back the door and peered inside. The closet was almost as bad as the laundry basket. She cringed and took a deep breath. It wasn't pretty, but she didn't have any other options. After a quick search she found the light switch and flipped it on. The closet didn't look any better with the light on. However, she did notice an abandoned banana peel which was better than coming across it by touching it.

Section by section Jo sorted through everything in the bottom of the closet. All she managed to discover was that Kent didn't believe in hangers. As she emerged from the closet she had to fight the urge to toss the banana peel in the garbage. Everything needed to remain the way it was. She left the bedroom and headed out to the living room. On the way she passed by a computer. The screensaver was on and caught her attention as it was filled with pictures. One of the pictures featured the restaurant they were at earlier that day. Kent stood beside the bar with a big grin, as the bartender rested a hand on his shoulder with a thumbs up. Behind them a television screen displayed a baseball game. Jo studied the picture for a long moment. For some reason that she couldn't pinpoint it held her attention. She snapped a picture of it with her cell phone, then continued her search. Luckily, the rest of the house was not as cluttered as his bedroom.

Jo rummaged through the kitchen drawers in search of the keycard. All she found were some coasters from the restaurant, bottle openers, and old paper clips. Nothing that would incriminate Kent. Her heart sank as she realized that she was going to end up with nothing from her search. Just when she decided to take another look at the bedroom, her phone buzzed with a text. Kent's car was on the move. She headed for the balcony. Along the way she double-checked to make sure that she didn't leave anything out of place. By the time she was on the ground again, Samantha was there to meet her.

"It was a false alarm, I'm sorry. He went in a

different direction."

"That's all right. Should I go back in?"

"No, it's too risky, you've already been in once."

"I didn't find anything." Jo frowned. "I'm sorry."

"Maybe there was nothing to find. We don't know for sure that Kent is the murderer after all," Samantha said.

"Why does it feel like we keep running into brick walls?" Jo narrowed her eyes. "I think there is a lot more to this case than we are seeing."

"It would be a good idea to regroup and review what we know. We should see if Walt can meet up with us. I don't want him to feel too left out." The two women met Eddy at the bus stop.

"Nothing." Jo shook her head. "I'm sorry."

"Don't be. If you say there was nothing, then there was nothing." Eddy met her eyes. "I know what a good job you do."

"Samantha thinks we should have a meeting."

"Let's do that. I'll try to get hold of Chris for an update. Let's say, half hour, my place?" Eddy looked between them.

"Yes, I'll catch a ride with Jo, if that's okay, Jo?" Samantha glanced at her.

"Sure that's fine. It'll give us some time to review things."

"I'll text Walt." Eddy tapped at his phone as he walked back towards the car.

Walt meeting at my house in thirty.

He sent the text then climbed into the car. He expected Walt to text him right back. When he didn't, he was a little surprised. Eddy started the car and drove back towards Sage Gardens. When he reached his driveway he received a text in return.

Be there as soon as I can.

Eddy raised an eyebrow. He wondered what that meant. Walt was only a few villas down, how long could it take him to get there? He dialed Chris' number. After a few rings Chris answered the phone.

"Eddy?"

"Chris, I just wanted to see if there is any new information on the case. I wanted to check if they have their sights on anyone?"

"Honestly, from what I can tell they are chasing their tails. Everyone has an alibi which makes pinpointing a suspect pretty difficult."

"What about Kent? Are they looking into him? I'm pretty sure he had something to do with it."

"You say he might be a suspect, but so far the detective hasn't figured that out. Right now he's their hero and only potential witness. He's not even considered a suspect."

"They are really dragging their feet on this one aren't they?"

"They're just being very, very careful. One mistake on this kind of case can ruin a detective's career."

"Well, one mistake could ruin my friend's life."

"Then it's good that they're being careful."

"I suppose. Let me know if you hear anything, Chris."

"You know I will. Keep me up to date too, Eddy."

Eddy thought about the break-in they had just conducted. He smiled to himself. Some things Chris was better off not knowing. "Sure will, Chris." After he hung up the phone he grabbed some food to prepare a sandwich. Walt's text still stuck out in his mind. He wondered just what his friend was up to.

Chapter Thirteen

Walt arrived at the restaurant with tension in his chest. It was so heavy that he considered taking a detour to the emergency room. However, he convinced himself that it was statistically more likely that it was anxiety. After a few steady breaths he parked outside the restaurant. As he walked up to the door he wondered if she would be there. Why would she be? She had no reason to have dinner with him. His suspicions began to rise. Was she trying to throw him off the investigation by pretending to be interested? The thought caused the tension in his chest to grow even heavier. When he opened the door to the restaurant he spotted her right away. After another deep breath he walked inside. She smiled as he walked up to her.

"Right on time, just as I expected."

"You're early." He sat down across from her.

"I didn't want to miss you."

"Oh, and why is that?" He looked across the table at her.

"I'm sorry? I'm not sure that I understand the question."

"It seems far too important to you to have dinner with me. So, what's the catch?"

She narrowed her eyes. "You like to get straight to the point don't you?"

"I don't like to be manipulated." Walt locked eyes with her. "Either you tell me what you want from me, or I get up and leave." The words sprang from his lips faster than he expected. He frowned. "I mean, there's no point in us wasting our time here."

"Walt, this isn't like you. Is something wrong?"

"All due respect, Madeline, but you can't possibly know what is like me. It's been years, and even when we knew each other, we didn't know each other that well."

"Maybe you didn't know me very well, but I

180

admired you from afar for some time. Either way, Walt, it's out of character for you." She tilted her head to the side. "Am I wrong?"

Walt sighed and met her eyes. "Can you just tell me why we're really here?"

"I'm trying to do just that. I invited you to dinner because I wanted to spend some time with you, Walt. But it is true that there is something specific I want to discuss with you, while we share a meal."

"What is it?" He waved away the waiter that approached.

"It's about Magnus."

"I knew it." He sighed.

"Listen, it's not what you think. I want to share something with you because I know that you can get to the bottom of it."

Walt smoothed out the napkin on the table beside him. He evened out the edge of the tablecloth. "Tell me."

"Can't we order first?"

"Please, Madeline. I don't do well with uncertainty."

"Okay. Here is the situation. Hiller Brothers has been a long term customer. However, when Mr. Hiller branched out and opened Hiller Maximum, Magnus refused to sign a contract with it, because the company was so small. I think he was hoping it would fail, as he did all small companies."

"Why is this so important?"

"I heard about the four digit number written on that piece of paper along with your name."

"Yes, we think it might be Kent's employee number. If you read the four digits upside down it's 9889."

"Well, that is one possibility. However, there is another."

"What?" Walt narrowed his eyes.

"We often label our different contracts with

the last four digits of their customer number. As I was reviewing some records I came across those four numbers. They belong to Hiller Brothers."

"Okay." Walt looked puzzled. "I'm not sure how it's relevant."

"That's just it, neither am I. Clive Hiller has always paid on time. In fact I don't even pay that much attention to his account because it is always paid. However, when I checked into his account I discovered that he has quite a large outstanding balance."

"Oh? That's very interesting. A balance like that might be a good reason to break into the computer system."

"Yes, it might be," she agreed. "I'd never suspect Clive of something like this, but I don't know what else to think. Maybe he was angry that Magnus refused to work with his smaller company and so he stopped making his payments. Maybe he was upset with Magnus for other reasons. I thought about reaching out to him, but

I decided to speak to you about it first. I don't want to do anything to harm the investigation."

"What about the police? Have you talked to them about this yet?"

"No, not yet. Like I said, Clive Hiller has always been a loyal customer. I would rather not bring the police into it unless we know for certain that he was involved. That's why I came to you with it. I know that you and your friends can be subtle about your investigation. You have that woman, what's her name?"

"Samantha? Jo?"

"The one that used to be a reporter."

"Samantha. How did you know that?"

"You're not the only one that can do a little detective work, Walt. I wanted to be sure that I could trust them, and you."

"I see." Walt sat back in his chair and stared at her. "I guess I have the same concern about you."

"As you should. It's been years. We don't know each other very well. But I'd like to change that. I wish this mess wasn't the reason that we were drawn back together, but I'd love for it to be an opportunity to start something new."

Walt smiled. He nodded to the waiter that approached. "Well, now is as good a time as any to get to know each other, right?"

"Absolutely."

After they had ordered their meals, Walt tried to sort through his thoughts. Every time he looked up at Madeline, all of his concern disappeared. It was a very strange sensation. Once the waiter walked away he met her eyes.

"So you think that Clive Hiller is involved, but not that he's the killer?"

"I doubt he'd ever get his hands dirty. But I also don't think he would order the murder. I don't know. I have this feeling that he's involved, but I just can't figure out how."

"Do you know him well?"

"No, I wouldn't say that. I barely know him at all."

"After all these years?"

"He's a private man. And there was some tension between Hiller and Magnus."

"What kind of tension?"

"Magnus considered him competition. It's not like their businesses were in competition, it was more like he and Clive Hiller were in competition, in life. I think there was some issue between Clive and Magnus' wife."

"Oh? That might be motive enough then."

"No, I don't think so. It was nothing more than a fling really, before they even went out. Not something that would have lasted over the years. It's just that Magnus took things so personally. You remember the way he blew up when he thought someone was stealing from him."

"Yes, I remember." Walt scowled. "I'd call him a passionate man if I didn't know better."

186

"Yes, he was just plain angry. But he's gone now. So it doesn't matter anymore."

"Madeline, what were things like between the two of you? I always worried about you."

"I can handle myself, Walt, I could then, and I can now. But it is nice to be worried about sometimes."

As they finished their meal Walt wiped his mouth and excused himself from the table.

"Just need to wash up." As he headed for the bathroom his phone buzzed with a text from Eddy. He sent a quick text back, then stepped into the bathroom. As he scrubbed his hands he wondered if he should tell Eddy about his dinner with Madeline. He really didn't want to. He didn't want to give Eddy any more reason to suspect Madeline. When he returned to the table he found Madeline signing a receipt.

"Madeline? You didn't pay did you?"

"Of course I did. I invited you, didn't I?"

"Madeline, I wish you hadn't done that."

187

"Walt, I enjoyed your company, and I hope that we can do this again some time. You can pick up the tab next time."

Walt frowned. He wanted to argue the point, but Madeline was already on her feet. "Let me know if you find out anything. Please, do me the favor of coming to me before you go to anyone else. Can you do that for me, Walt?"

"Yes." He met her eyes. "I can do that."

"Thank you." She offered him her arm. He took it and escorted her out of the restaurant. As they made their way towards the parking lot he turned towards her.

"Thank you for trusting me with this, Madeline."

"Walt, we don't know each other very well I know that, but I've always felt I could trust you with anything. Good luck on the investigation." She leaned in close and kissed his cheek. Walt flushed and reached for the tissue in his pocket. But instead of wiping his cheek he put the tissue

188

back and left the remnants of her lipstick there.

Chapter Fourteen

"Seriously? Where is he?" Eddy looked at his watch again. "It's not like Walt to be this late. Or late at all for that matter."

"He's not technically late, relax Eddy." Samantha rolled her eyes. "Your pacing is giving me a headache."

"I wouldn't be pacing if Walt would just show up."

"Sit down, please." Samantha pushed a chair out for him to sit on. Eddy glared at it and continued to pace.

"Here, try him on mine." Jo handed Samantha her phone. "Maybe he just needs to know we're all waiting for him."

Samantha nodded and dialed Walt's number. When he didn't answer she lowered the phone and caught sight of a photograph on the screen.

"What is this on your phone, Jo?" Samantha

stared at the picture.

"Oh, that was a snapshot I took of a photograph I saw in Kent's house. It was a screensaver on his computer. I don't know why, but for some reason it caught my attention. I figured I would look at it later to figure it out."

"I think I can tell you why." Samantha stared at the image.

"Well?" Jo leaned down beside her.

"This photograph was taken during a game that was played during the evening. Maybe it was a night that Kent should have been working. Let me see if my friend in IT can find out from the computer systems he's managed to access."

"Great eye. I never would have figured that out," Jo said.

"You knew enough to take the picture." Samantha looked up at her with a smile. "That's the only way we would have this to look into."

"All right, I know when to accept a compliment." Jo grinned.

"It doesn't mean much unless we can prove it." Eddy peered over Samantha's shoulder at the phone.

"Oh, I will, it should only take me a few minutes." While Samantha tapped away at the buttons on her own phone, Eddy finally sat down.

"What's bothering you so much, Eddy?" Jo locked her eyes to his. "You've been on edge ever since we started looking into this murder."

"I don't like the idea of prison hanging over the head of a friend of mine. It really bothers me when an innocent person gets caught up in some criminal's web."

"That makes sense, Eddy, but it comes across as if you're angry at Walt."

"I'm not angry. But I can't get past this feeling that he's hiding something."

"Listen up." Samantha had a triumphant smile on her lips. "We were right. He should have been on shift during that game and he only gets a couple of fifteen minute breaks. He wouldn't have enough time to go to the restaurant and be back in fifteen minutes even if he didn't eat anything there."

"So, what does that mean? Did he call out sick?" Eddy asked.

"No, there's no record of that. Maybe Kent has made it a habit of leaving his post for dinner on a regular basis, and not clocking out."

"He's sneaking around." Jo snapped her fingers.

"He might not have been at the company at all when Magnus was killed. Maybe, he was out enjoying a drink at the bar when it all went down," Samantha suggested.

"But he said he was attacked. Why would he lie about that?" Jo asked.

"To protect his job. If he slipped out when he should have been working then he likely didn't want to admit to that. Maybe he returned to the building, found Magnus dead, and concocted a story to cover up for his absence," Eddy said.

"Maybe." Jo pursed her lips. "All of his co-workers are calling him a hero, so he would want to keep up the lie now."

"Exactly," Samantha said.

"But there's another possibility," Jo suggested.

"What's that?" Samantha asked.

"Well, if he wasn't knocked out, he could have easily killed Magnus."

"You're right. We need to find out once and for all whether he was in that building at the time of the murder," Samantha said.

"Should we go back in for another search of his house?" Eddy asked.

"No, I have a better idea. Bartenders know everything, even things they don't realize they know," Samantha said. "I'm going to go in tonight and talk to the bartender that works the night shift. If that goes the way I hope then we might have something to work with."

"I could go with you." Jo offered.

"No, I'd rather go alone. It will be less conspicuous and hopefully the bartender will be more willing to talk to me," Samantha said.

"Trust me, you are much more approachable than me." Jo winked.

"Oh, you're approachable enough when you want to be." Samantha smiled.

"What do you think of this woman, Madeline, and Walt?" Jo turned to look at her. "Do you think he can remain objective?"

"I think, I've never seen Walt anything but objective," Samantha said. "He might be a bit enamored, but when it comes down to it, logic always wins out with Walt."

"Maybe. But he is still human, and pretty lonely," Jo said.

Samantha tilted her head from side to side. "I've never really thought of him as lonely. Now that you mention it, I suppose that he could be."

Eddy looked over at her as if he might have something to say, but Walt stepped in through the door before he could speak.

"Sorry I'm running behind, guys. What are we up to?" Walt asked.

"Kent might have lied about being knocked out because he skipped out of work to have dinner at the bar," Eddy said.

"Interesting." Walt looked thoughtful.

"Did you find anything?" Samantha asked.

"I noticed that there are small payments from Hiller Maximum going to Jimmy each month. I also want to look more into Hiller Brothers' accounts. I think Clive Hiller is going to be someone we need to look into."

"Maybe so." Eddy nodded. "For now I think we should focus on Kent. If we can confirm that he wasn't knocked out like he said he was the night of the murder then we have some real substance to move forward on. That way if the police attempt to make any move on you, Walt, we'll have something else to give them."

"So, you think Kent is lying?" Walt asked.

"We're pretty sure of it, because of this." Jo showed him the photograph of Kent at the restaurant when he should have been on shift. "That was taken when he was meant to be working. If he did it once, he could be doing it often or even every night."

"I'll go to the restaurant tonight, there's still time before it closes," Samantha said. "I'll see if he makes a habit of this."

"All right." Walt nodded. "I'll keep looking into Clive Hiller. I'm sure he's involved."

As everyone began to leave, Eddy walked over to Walt. "What were you up to this evening?"

"I'm sorry?" Walt glanced over at him.

"When I texted you, you said you would be here soon. I assumed you were out somewhere?"

"I was." Walt opened the door.

"So?"

Walt shrugged and stepped outside. He expected Eddy to follow. When he didn't, Walt closed the door behind him. Until things were clearer he wasn't going to give Eddy any more reason to doubt Madeline. If Eddy found out that she had fed him some information about Clive Hiller, then he would point it out as her attempt to deflect guilt. Walt hoped that wasn't the case.

Chapter Fifteen

Samantha sat down at the end of the bar. The rest of the bar was packed. She knew the bartender would be busy with those customers, but when he needed a break Samantha hoped that he would head down to the quieter end. From the distance Samantha could see that the bartender was the same one in the photograph.

As Samantha waited for the bartender's attention she looked up at the television and confirmed that it was in the same position as it was in the photograph. It was clear to her that when the picture was taken, not only was the night shift bartender on duty, but a game completed after nine o'clock was still on the television. When the bartender finally walked over Samantha slid a twenty across the smooth counter to him.

"What would you like?" He looked at the money, then up at Samantha.

"I don't want a drink, just a little information."

"Information about what?" He eyed the twenty again, but did not pick it up.

"About a man that frequents your restaurant." She held up her cell phone with an image of Kent on it. "Do you know him?"

"Kent? Sure. He's in here all the time. What kind of information do you need to know about him?"

"Well, I've heard a rumor that he comes in here, maybe when he should be at work. Do you know anything about that?'

"Oh." He shook his head. "I warned him that it was going to come back to bite him one of these days."

"What exactly?"

"Look, he's a decent guy, but he's tired of working night shift. He complains about it every time he's here. His boss refuses to move him to another shift, so Kent takes it out on him by

200

sneaking out of work. He comes here, eats a burger, watches some sports, and then heads back. It's never hurt anyone. I didn't think it was a big deal."

"It doesn't sound like it would be." Samantha shrugged. "Hey remember that game last week?"

"What game?" He glanced over at the crowd at the other end of the bar.

"The baseball game on Tuesday night."

"Oh, yeah sure. That was a crazy game."

"Was Kent here that night?"

"You bet he was. He was furious when the new coach put in that rookie."

"You're sure he was here?"

"No question." He laughed. "When Kent gets mad, you notice."

"Why is that? Is he violent?"

"Not violent exactly, but he likes to hit things."

"Punch?"

"No. You know, slam things." He smacked his hand hard against the top of the bar. Samantha jumped at the sound.

"Was he here the entire night?"

"No, just for about an hour."

"Do you know the times?"

"No way. Why do people keep asking me that?"

"People?"

"Sure, it's like all of a sudden Kent is the most popular guy in town. First, the old woman that always eats lunch here with her co-workers..."

"Madeline?"

"Maybe, I don't work the day shift much."

"And who else?'

"Some guy. He walked in here like he owned the place. When I didn't give him all the answers he wanted he got angry and left."

"Do you remember his name?"

"No, he didn't even order anything. I think I've seen him in here before though. I can't be sure, but I think it was with one of the baseball teams that sometimes comes in for dinner or a drink after the game. I think they might call him Hilly, but I'm not sure it might be a different person." The first thought that popped into Samantha's head was whether Hilly could be Clive Hiller.

"Do you know which team?"

"No, I don't know, I might be mistaken anyway."

"What about Kent, did you ever see him with Kent?"

"Look, I don't know what this is about but I'm too busy for this."

"I'm sorry, just one more question. How long was Kent here for?"

"It was a busy night. I barely had a chance to say hello to him. Kind of like tonight." He frowned as someone hollered for him. "Excuse me." As the bartender headed back to the crowd Samantha stared at the top of the bar. The sound of the man's slap still echoed through her mind. So Kent had lied about being knocked out, and he liked to strike out when he was angry. That added up to a very good chance that he was involved in Magnus' murder. She left another tip on the bar and headed out. As she walked to her car she dialed Eddy's phone number.

"What did you find out?"

"It looks like Kent is a liar, and has quite a temper according to the bartender. He was here the night of the murder."

"For how long?"

"I don't know. I can't confirm an exact time."

"Okay we'll work with what we have. I think it's time we paid Kent a visit."

"Don't you think it's a little too soon to tip him off that we're on to him?" Samantha asked.

"If Kent is volatile like the bartender claims, then we might be able to get him to lose his temper and confess. I think it's worth a chance."

"Tomorrow morning? We can hit him while he's sleepy, just after he gets off shift."

"Good idea," Eddy agreed.

***

Samantha held two cups of coffee as she waited for Eddy to arrive. They might only have a small window between the time Kent got off shift and the time he went to sleep. If they missed it, he probably wouldn't open the door. When Eddy finally pulled up, her palms were hot, and her irritation level was high.

"What took you so long?" She frowned.

"Sorry, got caught up on the phone with Chris, then straight after I hung up with him Walt called."

"Updates?" Samantha settled in and buckled her seatbelt.

"Chris let me know the reason that Kent's story wasn't investigated further is because the detective on the case was certain there would be video footage to prove his claim. There is only a video of the front entry and exit. By the time they realized that there was no footage, it was too late to have a medical exam done on Kent."

"But Kent still didn't insist on one, which is odd."

"Yes, it is," Eddy said. "I think you should let me speak first. I can be much more intimidating."

"But do we want him scared or talkative?" Samantha asked.

"Maybe a little of both. We'll start with one then shift to the other. But I'd like to take the lead." He pulled the car to a stop in a parking space in front of Kent's townhouse.

"All right, it's all yours." Samantha stepped out of the car. Eddy walked past her to the front door. He knocked hard on the door. A minute later Kent opened the door.

"What is it?" He rubbed his eye and squinted at them standing outside his door.

"Just need a minute of your time," Eddy said.

"I don't have a minute. I'm exhausted. You know, some people work nights."

"I'm aware of your schedule, I don't mean to intrude, but this is a rather pressing matter."

"What is it?" Kent frowned. "If it's about religion, you're out of luck."

"No, it's not about religion. Unless you count worshiping at a bar as your religion. Maybe that will get you out of the hot seat for leaving your post in the middle of your shift?"

"What are you talking about?" Kent straightened up. "I have no idea."

"No?" Samantha stepped forward. "I know that you are often clocked in at work, but are somehow simultaneously at the restaurant. How does that happen, Kent?"

"That's crazy. You can't prove that."

"There are many witnesses," Samantha said.

"So, you have a few options here," Eddy said. "Either we can take this information to your new boss, or we can take this to the police, who will find out that on the night of Magnus' murder you weren't knocked out and you weren't where you claimed to be. Or, you can answer a few questions for us."

He rolled his eyes and sighed. "Like you've never played hooky on a job.'"

"No son, my generation didn't do that." Eddy scowled at him. "So were you at the restaurant on the night of the murder, or weren't you?"

"I was at work for most of the time."

"But not at the time of the murder?" Samantha met his eyes.

"No. All right, no I wasn't there."

"But you found the body?" Samantha asked.

"When I came back, I saw him on the ground. I tried to help him, but he was already dead. I didn't know what to do. I called the police and then I panicked and I couldn't exactly say that I wasn't there, so when the police arrived I told them that I had been knocked out. I mean, nobody asked me to prove it."

"Unbelievable." Eddy shook his head. "Do you have any idea how much harm you did to the investigation?"

"I need my job. If I lose it, I'm going to be evicted. I made a mistake. I didn't kill anyone."

"Can you prove that?" Samantha took a step closer to him. "If you lied about being knocked out how do we know you didn't kill Magnus?"

"Why would I do that? He signs my paychecks."

"Your paychecks for the night shift, right?" Eddy squinted. "Isn't that a shift you've been trying to get taken off for a long time?"

"Look, I didn't kill anybody."

"How did you get in and out of the building without the cameras catching you?" Eddy asked.

"I went through the fire exit, the alarm on the door has been disabled."

"How do we know you didn't kill him when you came back?" Samantha asked.

"Look, I don't care what you do. Let the cops come, I didn't kill anyone. But first I need some sleep. So get out." He pushed his door closed. Samantha heard the click of the lock. Eddy raised his hand to knock again.

"No don't. We're done here." Samantha caught his hand at the wrist. "He's told us everything he's going to tell us. Now you need to let Chris know what we found."

"You think so?"

"Absolutely. If Chris finds out that you knew about this and didn't share the information with him then he's going to be very upset with you." She glanced at her phone as it began to ring. "It's Walt. Give Chris a call."

"Okay." Eddy walked back towards the car as he dialed Chris' number.

Samantha answered her phone.

"Walt?"

"I need to talk with you and Eddy. Can you stop by my villa?"

"Sure, no problem, we're on our way now."

Chapter Sixteen

Walt stared at the piece of paper in his hand. Just as Madeline had said, all of Clive Hiller's accounts were paid on time until he opened Hiller Maximum and Magnus refused to work with his new company. It seemed clear that he had withheld payment. Maybe out of revenge for both business and personal matters. Walt looked up when he heard a knock on the door. He opened it to find Jo on the other side.

"I came as soon as I got your text." He looked past her to see Eddy and Samantha headed towards the door.

"I need you to back me up on this one, Jo. Can you do that?"

"Sure." She frowned. "Why? Do you think Eddy won't?"

"I'm not sure."

"Hey Walt. What news do you have?" Eddy

stepped inside, with Samantha right behind him.

"It looks like Clive Hiller is our man," Walt said with confidence.

"Really?" Samantha raised an eyebrow. "He's such a powerful man to be concerned with such a thing."

"Powerful men like to get what they want, even if it means murder," Walt said.

"That is true." Jo nodded. "They tend to be sociopaths. That's how they get so successful."

"Not all of them I'm sure." Samantha shook her head.

"Take a look at what I found." Walt pointed out the debt owed to Magnus' company.

"What does this mean?" Eddy blinked as the numbers swirled in front of him.

"Clive Hiller was in the red, knowing that his account was in such good standing it wouldn't be noticed right away. Then maybe Magnus found out or Clive was worried he would find out so he tried to make it look as if he had made the repayments so that no one would know the difference."

"Wouldn't it throw up some red flags of some kind a long time ago if he wasn't repaying the money?" Eddy asked.

"Not in that particular system. The alerts were turned off for his account because he was such a good long term customer. Issues were supposed to be dealt with on a personal level so that there was no paper trail to embarrass him," Walt explained.

"I understand how you know about the transactions, but how do you know all of the other information?" Eddy narrowed his eyes.

"I have a source. I trust it. I think we should look into it."

"A source that you can't tell us about?" Eddy grimaced.

"Eddy, stop." Samantha shook her head. "If Walt says it's good information, then it's good information."

"Fine." Eddy nodded. "Then let's set up a meeting with Clive Hiller. Do you think you can help with that, Samantha?"

"I'm sure I can get that set up," Samantha said.

"I should be there." Walt frowned. "If this is about money, then I am the one most likely to be able to figure out and prove how Clive Hiller is connected to Magnus' murder."

"That I have to disagree with." Eddy shook his head. "You're going to be putting yourself in full view of the detective on this case if you begin having meetings with potential suspects."

Walt gritted his teeth. "I understand that, but it's still frustrating."

"Don't worry about it, Walt," Jo said. "You and I can look into Hiller's connection in other ways while Eddy and Samantha have their meeting. Sound good?"

"Sure." Walt sighed. "I guess I could go over

the financial records for his companies and see if I can find anything else."

"I might be able to help with that, too. Not the numbers of course, but I do know some ways he might be funneling the money." Jo smiled.

"Okay, I'll try to set up the meeting for tomorrow." Samantha pulled out her phone. "But if we're meeting with Clive Hiller, Eddy, you're going to have to look the part."

"I can handle that." He winked.

***

Early the next morning Samantha arrived at Eddy's villa. She walked up to the door anticipating one of his usual old, light brown suits. When Eddy opened the door what she saw was a tailored suit and a man she almost didn't recognize.

"See?" He smirked. "I told you I could handle

216

it."

In an attempt to hide her shock she reached up and straightened his tie. "You should wear a suit like this more often, Eddy. You clean up so nice."

"Flattery will get you nowhere, haven't you learned that yet, Samantha?"

"We'll see." She smiled and led him to the car. "Did you hear from Walt?"

"He just called to see what time we are going to visit Hiller. He's convinced the guy has something to do with the murder. He still wanted to go question him with us. I think I convinced him to leave it to us."

"You don't think he's on to something? I mean Hilly could be Clive Hiller and why would he be asking about Kent?"

"It could be but with Walt it's always about numbers. He sees something off about Hiller's finances, and he's going to fixate on that. But I fail to see why anyone as powerful and well off as

217

Clive Hiller would need to off someone like Magnus. Even if he did, I doubt that he would do it at his place of work. And again, I'm not seeing a motive."

"Maybe Walt sees something that you don't. He does have an eye for detail after all," Samantha said.

"Maybe. Or maybe he's just got tunnel vision. That happens sometimes too you know."

"I know, but we have to look into it for his sake."

"I agree, that's why we are going."

On the rest of the drive to Hiller's office Samantha gripped the steering wheel tight. She stared hard out through the windshield.

"All right, out with it, Samantha. I know you have something on your mind."

"How do you know me so well?"

"Just tell me what's bothering you," Eddy said. She parked the car in front of the large building and stepped out of the car. Eddy shut his door hard and looked across the top of the car at her. "What is it?"

"I just want you to be a little easier on Walt."

"Samantha, Walt and I are friends, he knows that I'm just looking out for him."

"Are you sure about that?"

"Look, just because we don't wash each others' hair and have pillow fights..."

"Really Eddy?"

He sighed and adjusted his hat. "What I mean is, women have a certain kind of relationship, and men have a different kind. Walt knows that I have his back, and that's all that matters."

"If you say so. We'd better get in there, or we're going to be late."

After a long walk through the lobby and a short ride in the elevator up to the second floor, they stepped out onto a carpeted hallway. As they approached a large, wooden door Samantha noticed a nameplate on the wall beside it. 'Clive Hiller'. It was a name she had done quite a bit of research on over the last couple of days. He wasn't just a wealthy man, he was a man of influence in the community. Hiller Brothers built strip malls, offices, houses and apartment buildings. Was she really going to walk in that office and accuse him of murder? She decided that she would have to be diplomatic. She knocked once on the door then opened it and stepped inside.

Clive Hiller stood up from behind his desk and smiled at Samantha as she walked up to him. His smile faded just a little as Eddy stepped in behind her.

"Welcome, please sit." He pointed out two chairs in front of his desk. "When my assistant told me that you needed this meeting today I made some adjustments to my schedule. But I'm afraid, I don't have very much time to talk. She said that you're interested in building a new apartment complex?"

Eddy looked over at Samantha with a cocked

eyebrow. Samantha stared directly at Hiller.

"Actually, that's not why we're here."

"No? Maybe I have the wrong appointment?"

"No, you don't. Please don't fault your assistant, I can be very convincing." Samantha smiled. "We only need a few minutes of your time, then we'll be out of your hair and you can continue with your regular schedule."

"What is this about?" Clive rested his hands on the top of his desk. He narrowed his eyes.

"As you may know a business associate of yours was murdered."

"Yes, I know that Magnus was killed. I've already spoken to a detective about it. So why do I need to speak to you about it?"

"We're consultants on the case. Hired by the family. We'd just like to gather as much information as possible," Samantha explained.

"I think you need to leave. You conned yourselves into my office, and I don't appreciate that."

"Please, Sir." Samantha offered a warm smile. "We just want to ask a few questions, then we'll be gone."

He sighed and shook his head. "Fine, what is it?"

"Did you know Magnus well?"

"Not at all. I didn't even like the man." He rolled his eyes. "Nor did I hate him, so please don't bark up that tree."

"What about his company? Did you ever have any financial issues with his company?"

"Not that I knew about. Somehow there was some kind of glitch in the software and my payments weren't being processed. But I only found out about that when the detective told me. I'm working on taking care of that situation now."

"With Jimmy?" Samantha asked.

"Yes, with Jimmy." He narrowed his eyes. "Why are you asking about Jimmy?"

"Are you aware that he is a suspect in Magnus' murder?" Eddy stepped forward.

"Jimmy?" Clive laughed. "Not a chance. Jimmy would never do that."

"So, you know Jimmy pretty well?" Samantha met his eyes. "Would you say that you're friends?"

"I would say that we've known each other for a long time. That's all."

"I suppose when Magnus refused to provide financial backing to Hiller Maximum, you were pretty angry." Samantha placed her hands on her hips. "Maybe you went to Jimmy about just how angry you were."

"Magnus was always trying to cause some kind of trouble. I was used to it. But Chad handled all of that. I didn't even know there was an issue for a while. By the time I found out, Chad was handling it."

"Seems to me that you don't know about a lot of things." Eddy rapped his knuckles on the desk. "Who exactly is Chad?" Eddy remembered that

Walt had asked specifically about two members of the baseball team. He was sure one of them was Chad.

"Chad is one of my employees. He is the companies' financial director and I recently appointed him as manager of Hiller Maximum so that I could continue to focus on Hiller Brothers. I don't expect to know about everything he does, but he and Jimmy were on the same baseball team and he did use Jimmy's financial advice on a few occasions for Hiller Maximum and paid him accordingly."

"So, the payments from Hiller Maximum to Jimmy were legitimate transactions?" Samantha asked.

"Yes, and I'm sure that you would know that if you were actually detectives, which you are not. So please, get out of my office."

"Sir, if I could..." Samantha began.

"No you certainly couldn't. Get out." He pointed to the door. "Or I will be placing a call to security."

"Mr. Hiller..."

"Samantha, that's it. The man wants us to leave, so we're leaving." Eddy started to turn towards the door. Samantha eyed him impatiently, but didn't argue. If there was one thing she'd learned about Eddy, it was that there was no point to arguing with him. Just as they reached the door Eddy paused and looked back at Clive. "I do hope you have a good lawyer, Mr. Hiller, because if everything you've told me is true, you're going to look mighty suspicious to that detective you spoke to. I came here to rule you out as a suspect, but I can guarantee you that the detective came here to rule you in."

"Well, you can both give up, because I have an alibi for that night. I wasn't even in the state. I was traveling to a conference."

"I assume you were with someone?" Samantha said.

"No, I wasn't," Clive replied.

"So, your alibi is that you were somewhere on the road all by yourself? You think that's going to stand up?" Samantha asked.

"Out!" Clive pointed at the door. "I don't have to answer to either of you."

"That's true." Samantha nodded. "We're not the ones with a warrant or handcuffs, but I'm sure it won't be long before they show up."

"I have nothing to hide."

"Then you should be willing to answer one last question." Samantha held his stare.

"What is that?" He sighed.

"Who else would want Magnus dead?"

"You say who else, as if I'm someone that wanted him dead. But I'm not. I might not have liked the man very much, but that doesn't mean that I wanted him dead. Business is business, I don't have to like the people I work with. As for who might want him dead, I'd say you don't have a piece of paper long enough to contain the list. Magnus made more enemies than any other man

I've known. He made most of his fortune from the failure of others. How well liked do you think he could be?"

"Thank you for your time." Samantha nodded. As they stepped out of the office Eddy looked over at her.

"Well, that was a bust," Eddy said.

"Not necessarily."

"What do you mean? We didn't get any new information."

"We know that it wasn't Clive."

"How? Because he claims he was traveling?" Eddy asked.

"No, because when I gave him the opportunity to point a finger at someone else, he didn't. A guilty man will always have someone in mind to pin the guilt on."

"I don't know about that," Eddy said.

"Really? With all of your experience?"

"Okay yes, usually a guilty man will try to

deflect his guilt, but maybe Clive is cleverer than that. He is the head of a million dollar company after all."

"A million dollar company that was still bullied and controlled by Magnus. Maybe Magnus was far more powerful than we realized," Samantha said. "There's no question that Hiller had the means and the motive to hire someone to take care of his problem for him. Maybe he didn't deliver the blow himself, but I think he may still be involved."

"You just said you thought he was innocent. Now, I'm confused." Eddy furrowed his brows.

"I said he might not be the killer. I don't think he did it himself. But that doesn't mean that he didn't hire someone to do it and maybe he believed that it could never be traced back to him. The important question is, did he hate Magnus enough to arrange his murder?" Samantha asked.

"Well, there was the matter of the overdrawn debt," Eddy said.

"And the interest that Magnus charged on it."

"It must have amounted to a lot of money."

"Maybe Hiller thought he could get a clean slate if he took out Magnus," Samantha suggested.

"Maybe, but it's a bit extreme, when Hiller has plenty of funds to cover the debt and make the monthly repayments," Eddy said.

"I think we need to find out if Jo and Walt found out anything about Hiller's finances."

"Hopefully they dug up something."

Chapter Seventeen

"What's this?" Jo stretched her arm over Walt's shoulder and pointed at the list of Hiller Brothers' account transactions.

"Hm?" Walt looked at the numbers. "What about it? It's a payment from a client."

"Are you sure?"

"Yes, I already vetted each of Hiller Brothers' clients to make sure that there weren't any fake ones. Everything in Clive Hiller's accounts seems to be flawless."

"Except that we know he was behind on his payments to Magnus."

"That's what I can't figure out. Why are there no transactions to cover that debt coming into Magnus' company? Wait a minute." He looked at the printout of financial records that Madeline had sent him. "Let's see, the amount is five thousand a month." He looked back at Hiller

Brothers' transactions. "There is a transaction once a month for that amount coming out of Hiller Brothers with a transaction notation of 'mag6886'. It must be for Magnus, but it isn't reaching the account. So where does that money go?"

He skimmed through the remainder of the transactions. As he searched, Samantha and Eddy arrived at the villa.

"Don't speak to him, he's working." Jo smiled. "He has me trained. How did the meeting go?"

"Not great. We're hoping that you found something." Samantha frowned and peered over Walt's shoulder.

Walt shook his head. "This is strange. The money goes out of Hiller Brothers' account but it disappears. It looks like the money has been taken right out of Hiller Brothers' account made out to Magnus' company, but I cannot see the payments going into Magnus' company. So who knows what happens to it after that."

"That is strange," Eddy said.

"I bet I know who is taking it and what happens to it." Walt rubbed his eyes then looked back at the papers. "I bet Clive Hiller is keeping it. That way he can claim there's a problem in the software, and that he's clearly made the payments."

"Maybe," Eddy said. "But that's a lot of trouble for a wealthy man to go to for a few thousand dollars."

Samantha stepped up to them.

"All right let's regroup. Here, we have Jimmy." She raised one finger in the air. "He has the most to gain from Magnus' death. He will most likely get the CEO position, which he has been after for quite some time."

"And here." Eddy held up a finger. "We have Kent, who claimed he was knocked out, but showed no injuries that would have been caused if he had been knocked out. He also had a problem with Magnus for keeping him on night shift. But as far as we know he wasn't even at the office at the time of the murder, unless he killed him before or after he went to dinner. Maybe he was caught by Magnus and they got in a fight."

"Let's not forget Madeline." Jo held up a finger as well. "Never underestimate the power of a woman's heartbreak. Maybe she was tired of waiting for Magnus to choose her."

"But the police believe the attacker was a man," Walt explained.

"That's true." Jo raised an eyebrow. "Maybe she hired a hitman. She could have been the one that let him into the building."

"Interesting." Samantha nodded.

"Let's not forget Clive Hiller. Somehow he's involved in all of this," Walt said.

"I know that you think that Walt, but I don't necessarily agree with you," Eddy said.

"Something is off about the money between these companies. How would Jimmy or Madeline stand to profit from that?" Walt asked.

"I don't know. But we need to focus on them and rule them out first," Eddy said. "I still can't believe that Hiller's motive would be a few thousand dollars a month."

"All right, I can't figure out Hiller's motive, yet. But it's often about the money. I really believe that we should take a look inside Hiller's home. Maybe we'll find something there," Walt said.

"No, I have to say no." Eddy shook his head.

"What? Why?" Walt stared at him. "What gives you the final say?"

Eddy narrowed his eyes. "Experience!"

"Boys, calm down." Jo lifted her hand to cut the tension between the two of them. "I am the one who gets the final say when it comes to breaking into someone's home. I don't think we should break into Hiller's. At least not yet. Not unless we don't have any other choice."

"Why not?" Walt frowned. "Because it's my idea?"

"No, don't be ridiculous. I just would prefer

not to break into Hiller's house because it is so high risk. He must have very high security and I wouldn't want to get caught. So, unless you plan on breaking in yourself, I think it's time that we change the subject."

Walt sat back against the chair. He wasn't happy that no one listened to his idea. But that was how it was from the start of the case. No one wanted to hear what he had to say. They believed that Walt needed to be protected and not openly involved in the investigation. He felt as if he was being treated like a child, when he should have been the one with the most insight into the case. Now that he'd been pushed aside yet again, he was sure that he had to find a way to prove his point. If Jo wouldn't break into the Hiller residence, then he would just have to find his own way in. As everyone began to leave, Eddy walked over to Walt.

"You know how much I value honesty, Walt, right?"

"Yes." Walt looked down at his hands.

"So, when I ask you this, I want you to be honest."

"Of course, Eddy." Walt looked up at him.

"Did you get this information from Madeline?"

Walt blinked slowly. His chest tightened. He couldn't bring himself to lie to Eddy. "Yes I did, at least some of it. We had dinner last night."

"That shouldn't have happened." Eddy grimaced. "Now we can't trust any of that information."

"That's ridiculous."

"So is making goo goo eyes at a possible murder suspect." Eddy turned and walked away from Walt before he could say anything more colorful. Walt stared after him and bit his own tongue. He wasn't a fan of losing his temper, but it certainly was boiling.

***

After everyone had left, Walt stared at the paper in front of him. He knew that he was right. He couldn't wait for Eddy to catch up and agree with him. Maybe he was an intelligent man when it came to detective work, but he didn't understand numbers the way that Walt did. He decided that he had to take matters into his own hands.

Although he had studied Jo's behavior, and her habits, he didn't think it would be enough to get him in the door. He could only hope that somehow he would get in. He knew he couldn't wait much longer for more information. He had to do something. He chose the darkest clothes he could find as Jo always wore black. But his were just a dark shade of brown. They would just have to do he decided. He put on his pants, shirt and sweater and his usual polished brown shoes. He tried to steady his breath as he grabbed some gloves from the top drawer and put them into his pocket. He still didn't know how he was going to get into the house. He had none of Jo's tools or experience. All he knew was that he had to try.

On his drive to Clive Hiller's house he tried to steady his hands. A couple of times he thought about turning the car around and heading back home, but he had to keep going. He knew Clive Hiller was involved but he needed the proof. He parked down a side street close to Hiller's house. From previous break-ins he knew he shouldn't park too close to the house, but he needed to be close enough so he could run to the car if he needed a quick getaway. As he put the car in park Walt took some deep breaths. When he finally had the courage he walked down the street and up the driveway to Hiller's house. There was no car parked in the driveway, but Walt noticed a garage to his left.

Walt didn't know what to do next so he decided to knock. If Hiller was home then he could talk to him and have a look around. He wasn't sure what he would say. Maybe he would pretend he was lost. Would Hiller know who Walt was and hurt him? Before he could think about it further he raised his hand to knock on the door. As his hand struck the door the door swung open. Walt waited for an alarm to sound. When it didn't he walked inside. Was Hiller home? Had Hiller left in a rush?

Walt slowly walked down the corridor expecting someone to jump out at him at any second. The first room he came across was Hiller's study. He slowly peered around the corner. He decided to go inside. Maybe he could find some documentation to prove that Hiller had wiped out his debt to Magnus' company and kept the money himself.

The moment Walt stepped in the room he heard someone approaching. He looked around for a place to hide. The only available space was a small closet with a slatted door. He ducked inside and pulled the door closed just before someone stepped inside the study. Walt held his breath. It was very difficult for him to do. The in and out pattern of breathing was a subtle routine that he counted on every second of every day. Now he held his breath in an attempt to keep his hiding place a secret.

Through the crack in the door Walt watched the man walk over to a bottle of gin and pour some into a small glass. He couldn't see his face properly, but he saw him swirl the liquid then sniff it. Walt had to breathe. He eased a breath past his lips as they trembled. No one knew he was there. No one would know if he disappeared.

Walt tightened his hands into fists at his sides. More than anything he wanted to burst out of the closet and attack the man. But he wasn't strong enough for that. He'd never been one for violence. The man turned, with the glass in his hand. To Walt's surprise he recognized him right away. It wasn't Hiller, as he had expected. It was Chad Hillwick. He lifted the glass to his lips and swallowed down every drop of the liquid. When Walt heard the clink of the glass being set back down on the silver tray his heart pounded so loud that he was sure that Chad heard it.

Chad walked towards the closet, his gaze focused on the slats. Walt tried to convince himself that Chad couldn't see him. He willed himself not to make the slightest sound. However, his throat began to tickle and he sensed a cough brewing. Just when he was sure he would burst out into a loud coughing fit, Chad turned and walked past the closet without even peeking into it. Walt exhaled and the cough began to bubble again. The closet door flew open and Walt dissolved into something between a scream and a coughing fit. Chad glared at him.

"I thought I heard a rat. I guess I was right." He grabbed Walt hard by the collar of his shirt and yanked him out of the closet. Walt lost his balance and crashed to his knees. As his hands met the carpet his mind raced with the amount of germs that he touched. But Chad demanded his attention with a swift kick to his ribs.

"What are you doing here, Walter Right? You should be in jail right now. At least there you would be safe."

Walt struggled to breathe over the sharp pain that carried through his side. "I don't know anything, Chad."

"Don't lie, Walt. You know my name." He rocked back on his heels as he looked down at Walt. "That's enough reason."

"You have one death on your hands, Chad, you don't need to do this."

"Actually, you're wrong. Magnus' death is not on my hands at all. It's on Jimmy's hands, or your hands, or even Madeline's hands, but not on mine, Walt. So, really I have no choice but to handle this situation, or it will be on my hands." He sighed and rubbed the back of his neck. "You should know that I had no intention of harming you. Well, other than sending you to prison for the rest of your life if that meant I wouldn't be a suspect. Really, how long do you have left anyway?" He chuckled. "I guess Madeline will have to take the fall for Magnus' death and yours. You know what they'll call her in prison?" He leaned down some and tried to meet Walt's eyes.

242

Every time Walt tried to get up he grimaced in pain. "A black widow. Every man she ever loved, ends up dead." He laughed. "Or maybe not. It's not like you two ever had the chance, did you?"

Walt stared up at him with disbelief. He tried to move his feet beneath him to get up, but Chad pulled back his foot and threatened to kick him again.

"How did you know about us?"

"She told me." Chad smirked. "I went to her, concerned about her because of Magnus' death, and we had a lovely chat. She told me all about your little investigation, and how she was sure that you would figure it out. The strange thing is, she even told me that she felt so lucky to have found you again. Now because of that luck, you're going to end up dead, she's going to end up in prison, and I, well, I will still be rich."

"I think that you're missing something very important, Chad. You should hear me out."

"I think you're just trying to delay the

243

inevitable, Walt. You're going to die. Do you really want to tell me some story before you do?"

"It's not a story." Walt narrowed his eyes. "It's a warning."

Chad crossed his arms and shook his head. "It's pathetic. You're just trying to distract me."

"What would that do for me? It's not as if it will save my life."

"Hm." Chad crouched down some. "What is it, old man?"

"I have friends." Walt smiled and looked into Chad's eyes. "And even when I'm dead, they will fight to find out the truth about what happened to me. They will seek justice."

"Oh please." Chad chuckled. "They know nothing about me. You don't think I noticed your surprise when you were hiding in that closet? I could see you the whole time. You weren't expecting me were you?" He shook his head. "Don't feel bad. That's the story of my life. Always underestimated. People just don't realize how smart I am. It's usually their downfall."

"Was it smart to steal from your boss who gave you an amazing opportunity to run your own business?"

"Oh sure. He threw me his scraps so I could beg at his feet. The moment Hiller Maximum met any trouble, it would have been shut down. Then I would be left with nothing, despite all of the effort that I put into getting that business off the ground."

"I guess you sensed your own failure when Magnus refused to work with you. Was that when you started to panic?"

"I didn't panic. Magnus wanted me to fail. He had set me up when I worked for him and then he thought I had failed him when I left his company. He wanted to buy Hiller Maximum out from under me and then eventually take over all of Hiller's companies."

"That's how you thank him for setting you up. By killing him?"

"Shut your mouth!" He slammed his foot into Walt's ribs once more. Walt groaned and tried to crawl away from him. Every movement caused pain. It occurred to him that these were the last moments of his life. He wasn't going to make it out alive. Every chance that he ever passed up for the sake of the safe choice rushed through his mind. Had he ever really lived in his tidy, secluded space? Was there anything that he could have done to alter this final circumstance? Chad grabbed him by the collar again and swept one hand underneath Walt's shoulder. He hoisted him to his feet as Walt screamed in pain.

"Quiet I said." Chad grabbed a towel from the small tray and shoved it in Walt's mouth. "No last words for you, Walt." He shoved him towards the hallway that led to the garage. "Can't have a mess on Hiller's carpet, now can we?"

Walt wondered if his threat would come true. Would his friends be able to figure out what happened to him or would Chad end up rich and happy as he had predicted. Perhaps if Walt hadn't been so stubborn, none of this would have happened. But it was too late to worry about that. The trunk of the car was open. Chad shoved him inside and slammed the lid shut. Walt hoped the journey wouldn't be long. Dread was an awful feeling.

Chapter Eighteen

Eddy frowned as he heard Walt's voicemail pick up yet again. Maybe the little spat they had earlier had more of an impact on Walt than he had thought. Was he too harsh? Walt had hidden his dinner with Madeline from him. It wasn't as if Eddy made that up. However, maybe it was wrong of him to question Walt's decision-making. Eddy cringed. He had a habit of questioning first and thinking it through later. He sighed and dialed Walt's number one more time. When he got Walt's voicemail again he gripped his phone so tight that he could have crushed it. He dialed Samantha's number straight away.

"Eddy?"

"Have you spoken to Walt?" Eddy asked.

"No. Have you spoken to him?"

"No. So you haven't heard from him at all?"

"I'm starting to get a little worried. It's not like

Walt to go so quiet."

"Something happened between us. I think maybe I caused this silence," Eddy said.

"What happened?"

"I found out that Walt had a dinner date with Madeline. He didn't tell any of us about it. I confronted him about it. I was worried that he was being manipulated by this woman."

"Oh Eddy, so what if Walt had dinner with her? They're old friends."

"So, maybe she was conning him."

"Eddy, I understand why you were suspicious of Madeline, but Walt has never given us a reason to doubt him. When you confronted him, you showed that you didn't trust him. No wonder he's not answering the phone."

"Now wait a minute, he's not answering your calls either. I didn't mention anything about you," Eddy said.

"I know he'll answer for Jo. Give me a few

minutes, and I'll call you back."

"All right, I'll be here."

Samantha hung up the phone then dialed Jo's number. "What's up, Samantha?"

"Eddy and I are having a hard time reaching Walt. We thought maybe you could try to call him."

"Me? What difference would that make?"

"He'll answer for you."

"Samantha, that's silly. Walt would answer for you or Eddy, too."

"No, I don't think he would. I think he's annoyed with us. He respects you, Jo, and he worries about you. If you call, I'm sure he will answer."

"All right fine I'll try, but I'm sure it's all some misunderstanding."

"Call me right back and let me know." A few minutes later her cell phone rang.

"Just like I told you. I called him and he didn't

answer."

"That's not okay. I know Walt, he never turns his phone off. There's no reason for him not to answer any of us."

"Maybe he's with Madeline."

"No. Something isn't right," Samantha said. "Can you come to my villa?"

"Yes. I'll be there in five minutes."

Samantha hung up and dialed Eddy's number. Before he could even speak she interrupted. "Eddy, get to my villa. We need to figure out where Walt is and fast. Something is wrong."

"I'll be there in a few minutes."

Once Samantha hung up the phone she sat down at the computer. With a few quick keystrokes she searched for a contact number for Madeline. She quickly dialed the number. Madeline answered after the third ring.

"This is Madeline."

"Madeline, my name is Samantha Smith."

"Walt's friend?"

"Yes. Have you seen or heard from him?"

The woman hesitated. Samantha could hear the heavy draw of her breath. She waited for a response.

"Is he missing?"

"He's not answering anyone's calls, which is very unusual for Walt. Did you speak to him today?"

"Walt's a private person," Madeline said.

"That may be, but not when it comes to us. I need to know if you hear from him, Madeline. I'm worried that he could be in some kind of trouble."

"I haven't heard from him." She sighed. "But, I have an idea of where he might be."

"Oh?"

"I think he might have been after Clive Hiller. He thought he was on to something. I don't know for sure if he went to speak to him and maybe see if he could take a look around his house, but he mentioned that he wanted to."

Samantha's heart sank as she recalled Jo's refusal to break into Hiller's place. Would Walt really have gone off on his own to do that?

"If you hear from him, please let me know. I'm very concerned about him."

"I will."

Samantha hung up the phone just as she heard a knock on the door. She rushed over and opened it to find both Eddy and Jo on the doorstep.

"I think we have a big problem."

"What is it?" Eddy frowned. "Did you hear from Walt?"

"No, but I did call Madeline. She thinks he might have tried to speak to Hiller and try to see if he could find any evidence. I think that maybe he even tried to break in, since we refused to."

"Walt." Eddy groaned.

"What is he thinking?" Jo shook her head.

"He's thinking that he wants to solve the case. Let's just hope that he has his phone turned off for that reason, and not because he's been harmed in any way," Samantha said.

"What are we going to do?" Eddy lifted his hat and ran his hand back across his head. "We don't even know if he really went after Hiller."

"I know one thing we can do. We'll go to Hiller's place and I'll break in if necessary. If Walt was there, I'll know it," Jo said.

"But Jo you said..."

"I know what I said, and now things are different. Walt's life might be at stake. I'm willing to risk whatever I have to, to find him."

"Let's go." Eddy nodded.

Chapter Nineteen

Jo fiddled with the window. It was harder to get into Hiller's than she had anticipated. However, with a little patience and a good tool she was able to break through the lock on the window without setting off the alarm. Once she had the window open she slid inside. As soon as her feet touched the floor she raced for the alarm to shut it off. However, when she reached the panel by the door she was surprised to see that it was already off. Had Walt turned it off or was someone home in the Hiller residence?

Jo flattened herself against the wall and edged along the hallway until she reached another room that had its door open. It looked like a study. Inside she saw a tray with glasses on it. One looked like it had recently been used. She knew that Walt wasn't one to partake, especially while breaking into a house. Someone was there, recently. Did they find Walt? Or was Walt scared off? She gritted her teeth as she reminded herself that she had no idea if Walt had ever even been there.

As Jo started to walk through the room she noticed that a corner of the rug was curled up. The closet door hung open. From the indentations on the rug it looked as if the couch had been shoved a little. Her heart sank as she realized that there had been an altercation in the room. When she saw a pack of antibacterial wipes on the floor near the closet her heartbeat quickened. That meant that Walt had been there, and since he hadn't called any of them, it was likely that someone did something to harm him. Jo rushed to search the rest of the house for clues as to where he might be, but before she could get anywhere her phone buzzed with a text from Samantha.

Hiller is in the driveway.

Jo's throat tightened. There wasn't time to

hide, she had to make a bold escape. In the middle of the hallway there was only one place to escape through, a door that led out to the garage. She hurried through it and closed the door behind her. As she drew in a heavy breath to calm herself, she noticed that the garage was empty. On the concrete floor was a stain that was still wet. A car had been there recently. She crept closer to the stain. Jo stared at it. A moment later she slipped through the garage door that led outside. When she joined Samantha at the car she was out of breath.

"I'm sorry I couldn't give you more warning, Jo, Hiller came out of nowhere."

"Don't worry about that. We need to find Walt. Someone took him."

"What? Do you know that for sure?"

"I can't be positive, but there was a fight inside of that house, and a car recently left that garage. I also saw antibacterial wipes on the floor in the area where it looks like there was a fight. I don't know for certain, but I have a very strong feeling that whoever was here took Walt."

"Was there any sign of injury?" Samantha held her breath.

"Not that I saw. But you know Walt would have put up a fight if anyone touched him."

"Yes." Samantha frowned. "We need to get the police involved."

"Why?" Eddy walked up to them. "What did you find?"

"It's what she didn't find. Walt is gone, and Jo thinks someone took him."

"Who? It couldn't be Hiller, he just arrived."

"Unless he's left him somewhere. I don't know who else it could be." Jo frowned. "How can we even begin to look for him if we have no idea who took him?"

Samantha grimaced. Then she glanced at the road in front of Hiller's house. Across the street was a mansion with several cameras pointed at the front door and street.

"I think I know how we can find out. Jo, are you up for one more break-in?"

Jo nodded. "Anything for Walt."

"Even a mansion with security cameras and eight foot high walls?" She pointed to the camera.

"Oh." Jo smirked. "My specialty."

"Enough of that." Eddy shook his head. "I can't allow this. That's too big of a risk."

Just as Jo opened her mouth to protest against his declaration, the sound of police sirens filled the air.

"See?" Eddy narrowed his eyes and ushered them both out of view before the police car squealed to a stop. Clive Hiller walked out of the house and met the officer at the end of the driveway.

"I don't know what happened, but when I arrived my alarm was off, it looks like there's been a scuffle inside, things are out of place."

"Someone broke in?"

"It seems that way, but I don't see how. There are no broken windows and the doors weren't forced open."

"Did anyone else have a key or access to your security system?" The officer asked.

Clive shook his head, then frowned.

"Actually, yes. I gave a key and the code to one of my employees earlier today. I asked him to stop off and get some records from my home office."

"What's this employee's name?"

"Hilly, sorry I mean Chad Hillwick. Actually, he manages one of my smaller companies." Samantha's eyes widened. Hilly was the person asking about Kent.

"Do you have any reason to suspect he's responsible for this?"

"Maybe he just had a hard time finding the files, and made a mess looking for them. I guess he forgot to turn the alarm back on. I'm sorry, officer. I think I may have wasted your time."

"Why don't you give him a call, just to be sure?"

"Good idea." He pulled out his phone. As the officer waited he dialed the number. After a few seconds he shook his head. "He's not answering."

"Well, then we can't be sure what happened here. I'll get some crime techs to look the place over if you'd like."

"Do you think it's really necessary?"

"Yes I do. Do you trust this Chad?"

"Sure. I guess." He shrugged. "We've known each other for a long time."

"Well, it's still better to be safe."

"All right, that's fine. I'll keep trying to reach him." He put his phone back to his ear.

Samantha tugged on Eddy's arm.

"I know that name, Eddy. He was on Jimmy's baseball team. He's an ex-employee. That must be who he's with."

"Yes, Walt asked me to ask Chris about him, but we crossed him off the suspect list because he has an alibi." Eddy grimaced. "He was at the baseball dinner with Jimmy."

"The bartender also said a man named Hilly was asking about Kent, too. I thought that maybe it was Clive Hiller, but maybe it was Chad. He might have been trying to find out when Kent went to the bar or if Kent actually saw anything the night of the murder."

"It's the best lead we have," Eddy replied.

"Maybe I can find out some information about him." Samantha pulled out her phone.

"No, that's going to take too long. Let me call Chris." Eddy dialed the number before Samantha even had a chance to object. "Chris?"

"Eddy, I'm off tonight. My one night off, in about ten days."

"Chris, I need a favor."

"Yes, I know that, Eddy. I know that every time you call me."

"Chris, I'm serious. This could be life or death." Eddy scowled.

"What is it?"

"I need you to find out what kind of car Chad Hillwick drives and his plates."

"Okay. Give me a minute."

"I thought you had the night off?"

"Like I ever take a night off when you're concerned, Eddy."

Eddy smiled. "That's what I like about you, Chris."

"No, you like all of the favors I do for you. Like this one. I'll text you the details. Why do you need the info?"

"I think he has Walt."

"What do you mean has him?"

"I think he's the murderer. I don't have time to explain now, Chris, but I need you to pull some strings and get a bolo out for this car."

"Eddy. I don't know."

"Chris, I know it's asking a lot. I wouldn't ask, but it's Walt."

"I just hope you know what you're doing."

"I do, I wouldn't be asking if I didn't. Can you let me know if anyone spots the car?"

"Yes, I'll text you any locations."

"Thank you, Chris. I owe you one."

"You owe me like three hundred. I'm still waiting on that steak dinner. Now, go find Walt."

Chris hung up the phone. Eddy turned to face Samantha and Jo.

"I have the details." Eddy flashed the screen of his phone towards them. "I don't know what else we can do right now. We have no way to find him until someone spots the car."

"I might have a way." Jo pulled out her phone and took Eddy's phone from him. She stepped away from Eddy and Samantha. After a few rings the line picked up. "I only have a minute. I need your help."

"Where were you when I needed you?" Jo immediately recognized the deep male voice.

"I was in jail."

"As if that's an excuse."

"It kind of is. But I don't have time to argue with you right now. You owe me, and I'm calling in the favor."

"I owe you." His voice darkened, then he sighed. "All right fine. But this is it. What do you want?"

"I need you to locate this car, and fast." She rattled off the plate number of Chad's car.

"It's only going to work if the car has GPS."

"I'm sure it does. It's a new model."

"I'll do what I can."

"Ben, I need this as soon as possible. A friend's life is at risk."

"So, now you have friends?'

"Are you going to help me out or not?"

"I didn't say no did I? Stay by your phone."

Jo frowned and tucked the phone back into her pocket. She turned back to find Samantha and Eddy closer than she expected. She handed Eddy back his phone.

"Who was that?" Eddy raised an eyebrow.

"Someone who can find the car."

"How?" Samantha queried.

"Does it really matter right now?" Jo looked between the two of them. "I was about to break into a mansion, I don't think we can rule out using illegal methods, do you?"

Eddy grimaced. "I can't believe that I let this happen. If Chad has Walt, he only has one thing in mind. We might already be too late."

"Don't say that." Samantha glared at him. "Don't even think it. Walt is the smartest man I know, he will find a way to keep himself alive. He knows we're coming for him."

"Does he?" Eddy shook his head. "I doubt it."

266

"He knows." Jo crossed her arms. Her phone rang. She grabbed the phone and put it to her ear just in time to hear an address before the line cut off. "Eddy, call one of your police contacts and give him this address, I have a feeling we're going to need back-up."

Chapter Twenty

The car lurched to a stop. Walt stared at the trunk above him. These were his final moments. He'd spent most of his life believing that if there was a problem there always had to be a solution. However, he couldn't find a solution to this problem. The trunk popped open and Chad reached inside. He clamped a hand over Walt's mouth, then wrapped his arm around his body. He jerked Walt out of the trunk and tossed him down on the ground in front of him.

"Help!" The shout that tore out of Walt was so rough and loud that his chest ached in reaction to it.

"Scream all you want. No one is going to hear you. Take a look." He pointed a finger over Walt's shoulder. Walt looked to see that he was crouched on his knees right in front of a huge landfill.

"Oh no, no, no." Walt tried to stand up. Chad kicked the backs of his knees. When he crashed back to the ground Walt tried not to touch the trash littered dirt, but he had no choice. Chad sighed and kicked dirt in Walt's direction.

"Stop whining."

"Not here, please, anywhere but here."

"Trust me, in a few minutes you won't care where you are, Walt." Chad pulled on gloves and looked over at Walt. "Just take it easy, all right?"

"Chad, this doesn't have to happen. Just think it through."

"That's the problem. I have no choice. There's no way I'm spending the rest of my life in jail, over a peon like you."

"It was you all the time, wasn't it?" Walt glared at him.

"What?" Chad raised an eyebrow.

"There's no point in pretending now. I know it was you."

"I have no idea what you're talking about."

"When I first worked for Magnus I pointed

out a flaw in his financial system. He never figured out who was responsible for it but it was you, wasn't it? You left before he found out it was you? That's why Hiller eventually gave you your own company, because you told him about the weak points in Magnus' system and you stole for him by altering the computer program so it gave his company discounts."

"You're a smart one, you know that? Too bad Magnus wasn't as smart as you. Back then, Clive treated me like a son. When I came to him with a way to get back at Magnus over some silly spat they had, he loved the idea. All it took was a little tweak in the computer system and voila, discounts on how much he had to repay for Hiller Brothers as well as a few other companies to avoid suspicion."

"Is that why Magnus refused to work with Hiller Maximum?"

"Magnus was clueless. He refused to work with me because he wanted to steal the company out from under me. But that didn't work out for him either, because I got Jimmy on my side, and Jimmy worked with me privately. He gave me all the connections to finance the company that I needed. I was always in charge of Hiller's accounts and so Hiller thought I was making the repayments to Magnus."

"But you didn't. You saw a chance to steal from Hiller."

"He stole from me first. The entire time he profited from the tweak on Magnus' financial program, he never once gave me a dime. So, I took the opportunity to get what was owed to me. I was meant to pay off the account for Hiller Brothers each month but I didn't. I just pocketed the money and let Hiller Brothers go into the red."

"But then things went south right? You knew Magnus would confront Hiller about his debt soon enough."

"Not if I eliminated it. Then no one would ever know."

"But Magnus caught you."

"Apparently, after you pointed out to him all those years ago that someone stole from him he got a little more paranoid. He installed a security system on his computers that alerted him if anything strange occurred. Since I logged in with your old login details, I guess that flagged it as a problem."

"So, the whole reason I'm involved in all of this is because of you? Were you trying to frame me?"

"Oh please. You're not that important, Walt. I needed employee details to get into the computer. I didn't want to use Jimmy's, even though I stole his keycard from him at the baseball dinner to get in the building. I was worried that if I used Jimmy's details or my old details it could get traced back to me. Lucky for me Magnus never updates anything, so your employee details were still active, and it got me into the system just fine."

"That's why he wrote down my name and Hiller Brothers' client number. But how could you have been at the dinner and killing Magnus at the same time?"

"I managed to slip out for a while. No one noticed. The only problem was I was delayed because I had to kill Magnus so I wasn't able to put the card back in Jimmy's wallet in time. If I did he would never have known that his card was missing."

"Why didn't Magnus write down your name?" Walt asked.

"He didn't even know it was me." Chad shrugged. "I heard him enter the office so I hid. When he walked up to look at the computer I hit him from behind."

Walt shook his head. "All for money."

"No, it's for much more than that. If Magnus found out I was stealing, then Jimmy would find out, and so would Hiller. Any one of them would have ruined me for much less. I had no intention of killing anyone, but Magnus just had to be paranoid, and really when you think about it, this is all your fault."

"Mine?" Walt's eyes widened. "How do you figure that?"

"If you had left it alone all those years ago, Magnus never would have realized that he had a thief in his midst, and he never would have installed the security program that alerted him and brought him to his death. I guess you could say, that this balances the books, doesn't it?" He smirked and pulled out a gun. "Now, I'd rather this wasn't messy. Have some dignity, old man."

Walt's heart raced as he stared at the barrel of the gun. He was sure that it would be the last thing he ever saw.

"Not so fast. Put the gun down now!"

Walt could barely make out Jo's voice over his panic. But there she was, just behind Chad. She had her hand shoved up hard against his back. Did she have a gun?

"Walk away, I don't need to kill you, too."

"You're not killing anyone. It's over, Chad. You're done for." She pushed her hand harder

274

into his back, but Walt couldn't make out what she held in it. "Put down the gun. I'm no cop, and that's my good friend that you have your gun pointed at. I'd have no problem taking you out."

Chad swallowed hard, then lowered the gun. Walt lunged forward and grabbed it out of his hand. His own hand shook as he grasped the gun. Loud sirens filled the otherwise quiet landfill. Eddy ran up to Jo's side and helped her wrestle Chad to the ground. Samantha took the gun from Walt and helped him to his feet.

"Are you okay? Did he hurt you?"

Walt stared into her eyes. "How did you find me?"

"Walt, we're your friends, we're always watching out for you," Samantha said.

Walt shook his head in a state of shock. "I thought it was over."

"It's not. You're okay." She handed the gun to a police officer, then steered Walt away from the chaos. She could feel the quakes that carried

275

through his body. "Here, I brought you something." She pressed a small bottle into his hand.

"Oh, thank you, Samantha!" He opened the hand sanitizer and squeezed a large amount onto his hands. As he cleansed his hands he looked up at her. "I still don't know how you guys figured out where I was."

"It took a little effort." Eddy frowned as he walked up to them. "And it never should have."

"I know." Walt sighed. "I messed up. I never should have gone in without letting someone else know."

"That's true." Eddy crossed his arms. "But I messed up, too. I never should have let you think that I didn't trust your instincts or opinions. Or that I thought you couldn't handle things with Madeline. I'm sorry for that, Walt. You deserved better from me."

Walt stared at him with disbelief. "You're apologizing to me after you just saved my life?"

"Technically, Jo saved it." Samantha winked.

"Jo! She can't have a gun, the police..." Walt said.

"Don't worry." Jo joined them. She waved a candy bar in front of him. "No gun, just chocolate, thought you might need a snack."

"Do you have any idea how much sugar is in that? Have you looked at the label?" Walt scrunched up his nose.

"Oh yeah, he's fine." Samantha laughed and clapped him on the back.

"I'm sure the detective will want to talk to you, Walt." Eddy remained by his side.

"I'm sure he will." Walt sighed and wiped his hands with hand sanitizer once more. "I just wish it didn't have to be here."

"Walt. I owe you an apology," Eddy said.

"No you don't, Eddy."

"Yes I do. If I had listened to you, and trusted your information you never would have gone off and done this by yourself."

"It was my risk to take."

"But you never should have felt like you had to take that risk. We're a team, Walt, and you're a very important part of it. I'm sorry that I'm used to playing leader, and I don't always give others a turn."

"It's okay, Eddy. Now that I've played leader, I'm pretty sure I'm going to let you have the role as often as you want."

Eddy smiled at him. "You did great, Pal. You saved the day, now the only question is, will you get the girl?"

Walt smiled and looked away as his cheeks grew hot. "I don't think I want the girl, Eddy. I am quite happy with the friends I already have."

The End

More Cozy Mysteries by Cindy Bell

Sage Gardens Cozy Mysteries

Birthdays Can Be Deadly

Money Can Be Deadly

Trust Can Be Deadly

Ties Can Be Deadly

Rocks Can Be Deadly

Chocolate Centered Cozy Mysteries

The Sweet Smell of Murder

A Deadly Delicious Delivery

Dune House Cozy Mysteries

Seaside Secrets

Boats and Bad Guys

Treasured History

Hidden Hideaways

Dodgy Dealings

Suspects and Surprises

Heavenly Highland Inn Cozy Mysteries

Murdering the Roses

Dead in the Daisies

Killing the Carnations

Drowning the Daffodils

Suffocating the Sunflowers

Books, Bullets and Blooms

A Deadly serious Gardening Contest

A Bridal Bouquet and a Body

Wendy the Wedding Planner Cozy Mysteries

Matrimony, Money and Murder

Chefs, Ceremonies and Crimes

Knives and Nuptials

Mice, Marriage and Murder

Bekki the Beautician Cozy Mysteries

Hairspray and Homicide

A Dyed Blonde and a Dead Body

Mascara and Murder

Pageant and Poison

Conditioner and a Corpse

Mistletoe, Makeup and Murder

Hairpin, Hair Dryer and Homicide

Blush, a Bride and a Body

Shampoo and a Stiff

Cosmetics, a Cruise and a Killer

Lipstick, a Long Iron and Lifeless

Camping, Concealer and Criminals

Treated and Dyed

Made in the USA
Monee, IL
12 April 2023